Revenge

Revenge

Bio-terrorism Unleashed

DR.NAVIN VIBHAKAR

PARTRIDGE
A Penguin Company

Partridge books may be ordered through booksellers or by contacting:

Partridge India
Penguin Books India Pvt.Ltd
11, Community Centre, Panchsheel Park, New Delhi 110017
India
www.partridgepublishing.com
Phone: 000.800.10062.62

Dedicated

To you which is yours,
To the pilot of the story,
to—my son
Dr. Rajeev Vibhakar.,

HEART FELT GRATITUDE

Of my wife, two sons, and two daughters in law as without their strong support this epic would not have seen a day light.

Of innumerable friends and readers from the literary world.

And to Pramesh Lakhia.

In event of endless sufferings, they become bearable only with one thought that, human life is very vast, very deep and has no end, while sufferings have an end and they will one day pass away.

Think of death, the death of which you are afraid. Just think what death is?

Death is the nature's effort to make life more strong and noteworthy.

Till the time your mind and my heart will not sail together, your mind will be busy calculating all and sundry, and, my mind will remain fogy.

**Living Voice of Khalil Gibran
—Dhumketu**

OUT BURST—PROLOGUE

Terrorism!

From where this ghost has come? India formed or allowed to be formed Pakistan by cutting right hand side of its head and right hand. But still Pakistan was not satisfied, Pakistan on two—three occasions declared war against India but did not succeed, and the end result is upsurge of ghost of terrorism. To save people from ghost the exorcist became active. But what even they can do? They do not treat ghost properly, but create mysterious atmosphere, create illusions and make efforts to drive away ghost. Keeping in view Pakistani terrorism I have written a novel titled as **"Shadyantra"**.

But question is where is the birth place of terrorism? Answer received is **"AL Qaeda"**. Again what type of ghost is it? And what all it does to create fright in people?. Their weapon is **"Jehad"** which is described in Holy Book of Koran as fight against injustice. It started misguiding people's blind faith in religion. When they could not survive in face to face war, they brought Neuro gas to suppress the revolt of Kurd people in Northern Iraq and killed about one hundred thousand people. As the proverb says "one who digs the pit, falls in it" and

America almost destroyed Iraq, and as a result Bio Terrorism started.

What is that—Bio Terrorism?

AL Qaeda brought Biological based virus into a reality. The question is how this killer virus kills people?

My elder son is in research work. He described to me this virus, and I got shivers. Can this ever happen? Its very thought was mind boggling, and while doing research he gave me the story plot of Virus (Ebola) and this novel got written.

Story got initiated in Urdu speaking nation and it has a global impact. The story was interwoven around Urdu speaking Muslim countries. As a result, based on my knowledge of Urdu Language and also doing research therein, I have used Urdu words in this book. Urdu speaking people should speak in Urdu while talking to each other is the purpose of my using Urdu words as a medium of my story.

The terrorism and bio terrorism got clubbed. The principal enemy of Al Qaeda is America. So story has a back ground of Uzbekistan. But terrorism spread to Russia. Africa and other Muslim Countries finally reaching to U.S.A.

Keeping this in view, it is important to read this novel. In India, Hindus and Muslims know each other since 1300 AD or even before that, so social problems covered in this novel will not remain unknown to Indian people because Hindus and Muslims are friends.

This is my first attempt to write such book a covering Muslims but I had my childhood in company of Muslims in Veraval a small town in Gujarat. In Africa, I had family relations with Muslims, so it was not difficult to understand their culture. America has Muslims from all countries of the world. This novel is written, with prime object to make people know that who all are affected by terrorism and about my outburst which I off load through this book. Bio Terrorism means terrorism spread through germs.

I hope that this book will be liked by all.

Dr. Navin Vibhakar,
64, Rock Creek Circle
Elton, Florida, 34222 U.S.A.
Email-navinvibhakar@hotmail.com

JEHAD\JIHAD

The word Jihad is an Arabic one. In Arabic language original name is Jahaad means the struggle, the fight against injustice.

Almost about 1400 years ago Prophet Mohammed gave the advice of Holy Book of Koran, which was written by Abraham. Since inception, this new beginning giving new direction, followers of Islam had to suffer a lot. They may be from Western countries or European countries such as Spain, Boznia or Chechenya.

In eyes of people, Islamic Religion and Jihad are very much blamed due to media coverage. The reason being ignorance of media about the religion. Jihaad does not mean terrorism but means fight against injustice. Some people have misused the same by making it a weapon which can be called terrorism but not Jihaad. Like Sanskrit, even Arabic language has many words which cannot have verbatim translation but is to be understood and experienced. Thus nearest translation of word Jihaad is fight against injustice without any self interest and having a philosophic outlook, forgetting the urge to have worldly comforts, riches and develop unity with God. This is what Holy Book of Koran said. "The importance of the later life is more important than just the birth". The Hereafter is far better for you than this life". (Koran verse 93:4).

God says. "Oh man folk. You do your best, I will also do. Finally you will be in a position to find out who is victorious. It is for certain that cunning people can never be victorious". Verse (6 :135).

Jihad is the symbol of Truthfulness. It is surrender to God and for that you may have to suffer a lot and that too you alone has to suffer. Only then God will forgive you. Holy Book of Koran describes this thing in following para.

"Every soul has to be one's own lawyer. You will get in return of your own deeds and that too here only, without any injustice". Verse (16:111).

"One day your good and bad deeds will be evaluated. God has said to do repentance for bad deeds. God is kind even to bad people".

Jihad is symbol of good deeds. Such as one does prayers or going to a Mosque. Do study Holy Book of Koran five times a day. Help the poor and the orphans, fight for independence, do not support liars, love your neighbors and friends. No stealing, no theft, not to insult any one and not to criticize anybody are the directives of Koran.

"Any woman or man who will live such a noble life will go to heaven". Verse (4:124).

God says "As for those who lead a righteous life male or female, while believing they enter Paradise without the slightest injustice." Verse (4:124).

For Jihad, justice is the main objective. Jihad means self defense, self protection independence for religious belief and need for justice.

"You should strive for the cause of God as you should strive for His cause." Verse (22:78).

Fight for God means fight for justice, Jihad is one battle. No one is prepared to understand the true meaning. But the meaning Holy Book of Koran is welfare and peace of mind and not war. The meaning of Arabic word Salaam is "Peace".

"You shall prepare for them all the power you can muster, and all the equipment you can mobilize, that you may frighten the enemies of God. Whatever you spend in the cause of God will be repaid to you generously, without the least injustice. If they restore to peace, so shall you and put your trust in God. He is the Hereafter, the Omniscient" Verse (8: 60-61).

Fight against tyranny, attacks and torture. For this Islam considers war a need based one. Even it considers the importance of peace on higher side, it does not encourage war but tells that the depressed ones to take the shelter of God.

"Those who really fight in the cause of God are those who forsake this world in favor of the Hereafter". Verse (4:74).

Islam prohibits barbaric war. Give respect even to the enemies. It prohibits killing innocent people. Fight only against those who have done injustice. Islam also prohibits people being enemies of each other.

"God advocates justice, charity. He forbids vice and transgression. He enlightens you that you may take need". Verse (16:90).

The meaning of this is to remove the wrong impression of the people and the media about Jihad.

It is made to understand that Jihad is a sacred religious war. But 'No'. In Islam war is kept at a safe distance. If no option is open and war may be a must, but even then to indulge in war is not considered sacred.

Islam means peace and delightfulness.

Jihad means to raise the voice against injustice.

"If they resort to peace, so shall you and put your trust in God. He is the Hereafter and Omniscient". Verse (8:611).

Keep faith in God. He is the new life. He is Omnipresent.

Courtesy—
Internet & Koran

CHAPTER I

Seeing the train stopping all of a sudden, he started thinking that even though Washington D.C. Station was very nearby why train stopped before reaching to the station, and, that too on the bridge of river Potomac?

He looked around in the coach. Nothing was unusual. There was anxiety on faces of all the passengers. He kept on holding his back pack quite firmly. The glass door from opposite side opened and he saw three persons and a woman in front entering the coach with pointed pistols in their hands.

Her womanhood was concealed in an agent's uniform. She had worn a cap. Having boycut hair style, she could not be identified as a woman. She came in front, and stopped near one passenger sitting in front row with a back pack, and said "F.B.I. Agent! Zeba Khalid". "Give me your back pack". That passenger gave her his back pack. Back pack was thoroughly searched from within. Except one book and few papers with notes nothing else was found.

But a man sitting in last seat in the coach startled hearing the name "Zeba Khalid" Muslim and F.B.I. Agent?. Why the back pack was asked for? Does she know? Quickly he opened the back pack and took out one syringe. He opened the cover of the needle and got up. While looking to rear door he put a step forward.

"Just stop there, I will shoot you" Saying this Zeba stood little away pointing pistol at him. Two agents came and stood at the rear door. There was no way to escape.

Being desperate he said "Being Muslim you are not giving support to Jehad?

"Do you say Terrorism to Jehad?"

"The war against Kafirs (non-believers) cannot be called Jehaad?"

"Whom do you call Kafirs (non-believers)"? To these innocent passengers? Innocent people? Does Holy Book of Koran teaches you this?" There was hatred in Zeba's voice. If you want to fight, do it face to face. By killing innocent people will your 'Jehaad' ever be successful?"

"But there will be an effect."

"To whom? To your companions? Or heads of your organization? You are educated, and your full biodata is with me. Terrorist organizations for their self interest make use of young and tender aged boys. Even that much you don't understand?"

"We are prepared to sacrifice ourselves for sake of our principle. You being a Muslim should support us."

"You have not read Holy Book of Koran in real spirit. It appears you have forgotten what your father has taught you in your childhood."

"What do you know about my father?"

"Seeing that the life of his only son going haywire he died because of affliction of his son's separation and remembering you every moment, even then you have not improved."

"I won't budge from my goal. If you will come closer to me, I will prick the syringe."

"You are not going to get that much time. In your back pack there are many syringes, and you want to make use of them in Washington isn't it? But now it will not happen. Keep your back pack down otherwise I will fire. There is no way for you to escape."

He looked in all directions. Everywhere F.B.I. agents have surrounded him. Helplessly he looked up and said.

"The Almighty-Allah will never forgive you" saying that he kept his back pack on the ground. He was hand cuffed.The train started. Passengers took a deep sigh of relief as if they have seen a thrilling movie which has just got over.

Moment the train reached Washington he already was handcuffed, and he looked to Zeba in totally helpless situation.

"You are forcing me to tell you all the facts, but agent Zeba, even though you are a Muslim lady you are still helping our enemy country? Such a country which is misusing its power? It is America. Why and for what you are doing such things?"

Shaikh Abi Salim of Kuwait read the message and started thinking. "Let Kuwait be a Dominion of Iraq. We will rule over the world by oil richness of our two countries" Reading this message from Sadaam he got wonder struck. All Islami nations were longing for mutual cooperation to spread Islam. While this message is to engulf the entire area. The message was put forth in Assembly. Which group of people or a nation will like to be a dominion?." Today was the last day to send the reply. Kuwait was quite wealthy but the country as such was quite small and tiny. It did not have any strength to stop aggression.

And before any help can be received, Iraq—Sadaam Hussain invaded Kuwait. But Abi Salim on the earlier night using his foresight, informed American Ambassador about Sadaam's attack.

Invasion had already taken place. Kuwait was about to lose its identity. At that time a message from President Bush was received. American sub marines have entered in the Bay of Kuwait. Aerial attack got commenced on Iraqi Troops.

"Jalal what shall we do? Amina's eyes were full of agony.

"Amina! We cannot stay here in this situation. Only yesterday American Ambassador informed me that our Visa calls are expected any moment."

"Yes but! In this war like situation how shall we get out? We cannot take anything from here ". Amina fondled little Zeba and said "Amen". Being desperate she said "Nothing is more important then the life, not even wealth."

Next day Jamal Shaikh went to meet American Ambassador Mr. Calahaan. Both were friends, Jamal was a chemical engineer "Oh Jamal! Thank God you came, your call is received."

Yes Sir! But how shall we go from here?

There are few other families like yours. Their Visas have been processed. Now you can be considered American Citizens. Your responsibility is our responsibility. Now I have talked to Homeland Security.

You all will be taken in U.S. War planes. Yes, but you have to leave all your belongings here only.

"But while going there our immediate . . . ."

"For that necessary arrangements have been made by our Church. Till the time you get a job, your shelter will continue. But yes! Are you a chemical engineer isn't it? How much you know of chemical weapons? I have already spoken to Homeland Security on this matter and seeing your bio data you have been appointed as a chemical engineer in Govt. Office. Mr. Charles Christie is head of Homeland Security. In case of need you can ask for help giving my reference ".

"Amin! Amin! God's blessings! Saying this entire Khalid family came to Washington in a war plane. Zeba was briefed in her childhood that you are duty bound to this country. After completing college education Jamal asked young Zeba "Dear! What are you future plans? Do you want to get engaged? Do you have anybody in mind or we start looking for you a good match?

With changing times the thinking of hard core parents staying in wealthy and modern country like America also change. It is the essence of change.

"No Papa (she used to say papa instead of Abba)" my desire is to join Homeland Security and work in Chemical and Biological Warfare department".

"In short, you want to be an FBI agent? Do you know it is very hard and difficult job?".

"Yes Papa! But I am ready, to pay all the gratitude to the country which made us their citizens ".

"Welcome, Dear! I will talk to Mr. Charles Christie."

"Sir, this is my young daughter Zeba, she is a graduate, she wants to work in your Chemical and Biological Warfare department and by making progress therein, she wants to be an agent."

"Mr. Khalid! Does she know how difficult is that job? Is she aware that she has to swear and take an oath and be away from the family for quite a long period?"

"Sir! Zeba interrupted" I will not fail short in discharging my duties as an American Citizen".

"One moment! Saying this Charles lifted the phone." Hello! is it Mr. Calahaan? You have called at an appropriate time." Saying this he told him about Khalid family.

"Mr. Christie! I give their guarantee."

There is no doubt for that matter. Mr. Khalid's research in chemical and biological field is matchless. Moreover one Indian Researcher appointed by him has done wonders. Now on conquering Kuwait, the committee that is going to examine chemical weapons of Sadaam, in that committee the names of Mr. Khalid and his assistant are already included. Now what remains is that of Zeba?

"That guarantee is also of mine" saying this Mr. Calahaan put down the phone ".

"Come on, your plea is approved."

"Sir! I won't fail you, You will not be disappointed even the least, that is my word." Zeba got up and said shaking her hand with him.

Mr. Charles Christie the head of Homeland Security looked at Zeba with sharp eyes and was thinking "will this soft looking young girl is seeing the dreams of becoming the agent which is very tough? Will she be in a position to take hard training? Will she be in a position to bear all such difficulties?"

And he said "Miss Khalid! It is not easy to be an agent. You have no idea of what all you have to do. Before joining any secret agency in the world you have to forget your dear ones. You have to do the hardest of hard jobs. Are you Muslim isn't it "? Saying this he looked to Khalid and said "You are a strong follower of your religion isn't it? Is it not so that in your religion character has been given the utmost importance? But by becoming a secret agent without caring for the self, one has to sacrifice everything to extract information. I have read good amount of material on Muslim and Hindu religion. When India was one and united Muslims have invaded. They were nurturing poisonous snakes to kill the enemy. In our spying agencies there is nothing of that type. You will be the boss in our spy organization. Yes, as per the rule you will get two weeks holidays in a year to go and meet your family. But during that period also you will be under our close watch. We have to see that the classified information of our country and the world you are having will not be misused. Many a time such agents have a mental break down. To such agents we treat separately. Will it be possible for you to observe all this?"

Zeba looked at him. He said "Miss Khalid Dear! How do you feel.? Do you want to join the fray by sacrificing your body, mind and religion "?

"Papa! this country has given me protection, has given me citizenship, has provided me education, would it have been possible for me to do all these without their help "?

"Dear! this society . . . ."

"Mr. Khalid! said Mr. Charles, "Yes, at this stage if miss Khalid gets enrolled as an agent, then this matter is to be kept secret. There is no need of getting afraid of society. As and when she will get assignment gradually she have to be away from the family. She can say to all others that she has gone away for further studies."

Zeba's face sparkled with enthusiasm ". Mr. Charles! Everything is fine. But you are giving treatment to agents having classified information what is that "?

Mr. Charles appreciatively looked to Zeba. "Bravo, you are smart and active ". I want to show you something. First have a look at it and then decide your line of action after having a look ".

"Have a look, means what?"

"I want to show you a film. But before that both of you have to take an oath that you will not talk anywhere about the film. Mr. Khalid not even to your wife. Do you agree?"

Both of them took oath and went to auditorium. It was dark and the words appeared on big screen.

"West Virginia"

Paris Island Psychiatric facility.

Hospital building was seen. The scene was that of the wards having the cells like prison rooms.

One man was there in a cell. "Mr. & Miss Khalid, this is agent James Campbell. He is under psychiatric treatment. Due to classified information of Iraq, Afghanistan, Iran gradually created stress in his mind and so a need to treat him was felt. This facility is of Homeland Security. He even does not remember why he is here. He became an agent when he was 22 years of age and today he is of 55 years old. Are you ready for this kind of situation? You will be considered "our property". It will be our responsibility to keep you fit. Moreover at times such patients try to run away from here. See further ".

With wide open eyes Zeba was watching how Campbell runs away from this island and reaches to his apartment in New York.

Only two years have passed on his treatment. It appears that every one has forgotten him. He went to a library, set on a computer and typed his name on State Department's data base and read.

"James Campbell not found" There is no data against this name. He got surprised. Therefore he typed his Social Security Number (Every one is given such numbers in America typing which the records of particular person is available) the reply was "James Campbell not found".

"Zeba and Mr. Khalid looked at Charles. Mr. Charles took a pause and said" Now you should have understood that the agent is our property. His total records are kept secret. It is not available to public or to the person himself." Mr. Khalid looked at his watch, Mr. Charles closed the film.

"We will see further some other time. I am giving you time to think again "No Sir". Zeba looked to her father and said "I will not allow such situation to arise in my life. I will protect my self on all counts" Zeba said this with firm determination.

"One more thing Miss Khalid even your private life will also be our property. Once you successfully come out in our mission only thereafter you can start your family life, or perhaps that moment may not come in your life at all ".

"That means"

"Are you in love?" . . . . stopping here he looked to Mr. Khalid. "In your religion such matters are not discussed in presence of father and the daughter. But this business is such."

"Mr. Charles! After staying in America our outlook towards the life and the style of living have undergone a change" said Mr. Khalid. "Yes Mr. Charles what were you saying?" asked Zeba.

"If you fall in love even at that time you will not talk about secret information and you will have to take an oath for this. If at all you say something you do not forget that you will always be under our watch".

"Then my life, my family?" Zeba asked at low voice.

"Don't be afraid. Before you reach to the level of "classified information" you will be consulted whether you want to get married or you want to proceed further for the job of an agent. For time being you will be trained in simple matters."

And as Zeba went on overcoming difficult challenges of FBI agent then she realized that why spying agencies have such an esteemed place. Today she has captured one Muslim Terrorist.

"Now tell me 'Ullug'! The country whom you consider an enemy, can that country be not more than a friend to me? Whom to consider a friend or an enemy that decision cannot be taken by an isolated incident.

Ullug got shaken and asked "Do you know about my experience?

Yes! I know, Tell me why a religious minded person like you become a terrorist?"

Ullug looking outside the window was in the same state of mind as he was when he went to Tashkent for the first time and looking outside the window, he got lost in thoughts and started narrating . . . .

CHAPTER 2

What will happen?
Will the reply be received?
Will the place be available?

Ullug was looking out of window from his poverty stricken poor house towards star studded dark night. From within, he was highly uncomfortable. His desires were boundless. His ambitions were filled with seven colors of Rainbow. His enthusiasm was waxing and wanning like sea waves. The fascination of young age was creating terbulence in his mind. His mind was full of darkness just like that of dark night, but still thoughts like sparkling stars were filing his mind with brightness.

Since quite a few nights this was a daily routine for him. He was a descendant of Changiskhan's grand son and daughter's son of Chugtai family. Alnashir Nawab was aware of the restlessness of his grand son. He was not in a position to see the misfortune of the descendant of Changiskhan who once ruled over the whole world. But what can be done? What all is not required to be done in case of slavery of a dependent nation? In fact Uzbekistan was now a Province of Russia, in fact a conquered country.

Since 1571, Russia was attacking Uzbekistan's rural border. But who can raise a voice against all powerful Russia? In fact Uzbekistan was surrounded by Kazekistan, Kirgistan, Tazikistan, and Afghanistan. One corner of Pakistan also was touching it. Emperors of the world were devotionally attached with Samarkand Bukhara. Beautiful and charming city of Tashkent is like the beauty spot of women. It also was a subordinate State of Russia.

But who can survive or endure against the time? Ismail Beg did upbringing of his son after his wife's death. As it happens that in a dependent nation facility for education is on lower side. Tashkent was a nice city. But Soviet Union by building the bridge of friendship and a rail road on the river Amuduria, extended its borders up to a border town Caliph of Afghanistan. At that time no one in the world had slightest idea about Soviet Union's intentions.

Though they were developing Tashkent, still no university was established in that town.

Ismail Beg after giving school education to his son, he encouraged Ullug for admission in Moscow University. Seeing his son's restlessness and ambitious eyes staring to the sky in dark nights, Ismail Beg was getting highly disturbed. But he had unflinching faith in God. From childhood he made Ullug to learn Holy Book of Koran and also the lessons of peace and prosperity. Ullug was becoming a religious minded person with pleasing nature and having love for education.

While applying, father and the son sitting on a small carpet were filing the application form. "My son I have not studied much. You are bright in studies. What are your future plans?"

"Abba jaan! After doing four year's course in college in Science subjects, I want to earn the name in Bio-chemical research."

"What is that my son?"

"Abba Jaan! (for daddy) These researches are for upliftment of mankind. Just like vaccines to cure the disease."

"If you get an admission in Moscow College then you have to go there isn't it?"

Ismail had tears in his eyes. Who else was there in his life? Will he be in a position to bear separation. But keeping in view his son's future he had to be strong mentally. How long will they live in poverty!. Being firm he said.

"But my son! How shall we manage to pay for research fees to the college?"

"! Do not worry, Abnajaan!. Keep faith in Allah (god). Mr. Alnashir, head master of my school has given me a recommendation letter on the Principal and Research Director Dr. Khoshev and simultaneously I have applied for scholarship too."

"If you have to go, where will you stay?"

"The stay in hostel will also be free if I get scholarship."

"Allah may give you all success. But my son! You know that we are from a small village. There are lot of temptations in cities, will you be in a position to take care of yourself?"

"Abbajaan! Can I be different from what I am today? YOU have raised me and taught me good values of life and our culture." His voice got emotionally choked. "you have never fallen short of mother's love. You could have married again, but you have not done that. I will not forget your sacrifice. It will not go unrewarded."

"Oh!my son," and he embraced him and said with love, "Allah will make you successful. Do not be restless. Go and sleep now.

Dr. Khoshev was in deep thoughts while sitting in his office. While reading about African countries, He thought there are many avenues which can be explored there for unique opportunities for research for new inventions. Soviet Union was trying to have a strong hold in African countries. Gradually a request for co-operation was received from an opposition party of country like Angola. During that time they came to know that in rain forests area on the border of Zaire and Tanzania Forest Park, one unknown disease had spread in Chimpanzees. In order to find out the germ-virus spreading the disease, countries of that area have asked the help of Research Dept. of Soviet Union. Countries like Africa of an undivided continent were gradually developing on getting independence. America still had reservations in going to those countries. Other countries were mostly colonies of Britain, France and Portugal. So countries from Africa inclined towards Soviet Union.

At that time he heard a knock on the door. Dr. Khoshev said "Come in".

In Communist Countries, word peon cannot be used. There, every one has equal rights. But in reality, it is slavery only. But under the cover of hypocrisy, Communist Govt. always used to project themselves good.

The messenger came in. He had two envelopes in his hand. He kept them on the table of Dr. Khoshev and quietly went away. Dr. Khoshev lifted one envelope. Reading the name of Alnashir, there was a smile on his face as both of them have studied together.

He opened the envelope.

"Khoshev! This is a personal letter, so I am writing to you in your first name. In enclosed envelope there is an application of one of my students. Consider him as my son. He is to be given admission in your research division for a six year's course.

He is 18 years old but he is very bright. In future he will not only make his name, but, will also brighten your name. Perhaps he will also be known all over the world. He has a bright career."

When are you coming to Tashkent? My house is your house. You know that many a times I recollect the days we have spent together during our student life.

For time being Good Bye . . . I look forward to have good news from you."

Khoshev opened second envelope. He read whole application. He was highly impressed. He felt that Alnashir's request was justified. Ullug was 18 years old. This is the year 1980. During that time, from 1979 as requested by Afghanistan, Democratic Republic Govt. of Soviet Union sent military aid for their help. Mujahuddins were asking help from other countries also to save Islamic religion. Countries like America, Saudi Arabia, Pakistan etc. had their self interest, but the neighbouring country for them was Soviet Union. Moreover boundaries of Uzbekistan and that of Afghanistan were touching each other. Just a step further. In 1979 Soviet Army entered in Afghanistan through Tashkent and Caliph. Who was knowing that this war in hilly areas will continue for nine long years?

Fresh wind came from the window. Papers of application started flying. Khoshev came out of thoughts and gathered the papers. One new thought sprang up in his mind.He concentrated on name of Ullug.

Reading the letter, Alnashir got up from his chair. He was sure that Ullug will get admission based on his recommendations, but arrangement for scholarship, absolute free education, and arrangement for stay and food were to be done as well."? "WHAT A DESTINY?" Feeling happy, he got up from his chair, and he sent for Ullug. Ullag's school was over and he was helping his father in his hand weaving business. The hand woven carpet of Ismail beg were very much liked by all. Sunnis were using his carpet only while doing prayer. Ismail Beg was getting his livelihood from the sale of carpets.

Hearing a knock on the door, Ullag got up leaving his work half done and opened the door. The messenger gave him an envelope. Ullag's heart beats increased. Even otherwise from where poor people get letters?

"Son! what is that?" while continuing weaving Ismail asked.

"ABBAJAAN! There is an envelope, I will open it and see."

"Son! It may be a reply of your application." Due to constant failures, the human mind loses power of thinking that anything good also can happen to them, and so the tone of Ismail was quite passive.

"Abbajaan! It is Alnashir Sir's note. He has called me immediately."

The anxious moments were extended for some more time.

"Son! Go fast! God must have sent good news for you" Ismail had tearful eyes, and, as if he was praying he raised his two hands and saw upwards making a humble request.

Ullug went running. He was breathless when he reached Alnashir's office. He reaching there, he knocked the door.

"Come in"

And seeing Ullug, Alanashir got up from the chair and came forward. He embraced his son like Ullug, and said "Come, Ullug come!"

Ullug's eyes were shining with eagerness like sparkling stars in a dark night. Alnashir could see many questions coming up in Ullug's dreamy eyes. Not making him wait any more, letter of Dr. Khoshev confirming his admission was kept in Ullug's hand. Ullug read the letter. His eyes were full of tears of happy moments. He got up and as if he was doing Namaaz—prayers, he sat on the floor to pray.

Alnashir got up and said, "Ullug! Sit comfortably. Look! There is also a personal letter of Dr. Khoshev on me. You may not be knowing but we were co-students and became friends. He is very close and loving friend of mine.

See! He has given free admission to you in a six year's course. Hostel accommodation is also free and for your food and provisions he has arranged in such a way that you will be getting cash money."

"Sir! this is only possible because of you."

"Ullug! Raising the finger towards the sky Alnashir said "Without His favour nothing moves."

"But Sir! For all these years I have not put my foot out of Tashkent. At present Russian army is moving every.where. How will I reach Moscow?" "Ullug! This is what is called luck. You are destined to earn a name. That is why God is doing all favours. Dr. Khoshev's daughter is getting married. I have received emotionally filled invitation. I must go to attend the marriage of my school friend's daughter, I have booked three train tickets, for me, my wife and you."

"But Sir! Ticket fare money . . . . from where shall I bring?" Ullug's voice got shaky. "Has any one asked money from you?. Do you know that by this admission you have dignified my name, our school's name and that of the whole town? Take this as an ordinary gift from us. And see, your Abba must be waiting for you to return. Do you know how anxious would he be?"

Ullug got up "Yes! But Sir! When will we be going?"

"I will let you know after everything is finalized. It will be about a week."

And Ullug started running closing his fists. What was there in his closed fists? Ullug's future? How was that future?

Breathless he came to his house and knocked the door "ABBA! Abba!!" HeariAng the fully excited voice of Ullug, Ismail got up.

"Oh God! Here also a failure?"

He got up. He took Ullug in his hands and while fondling him he said." Son! My son! Not to be afraid of failures. God is taking our test."

"No! No! ABBA!. It is not as you are thinking. I have got admission" and he told everything in detail. Ismail folding both the hands showing respect to Allah, set on a carpet.

"My son! God has done this much favour. Your dream has come true and you got the support of honest person like Alnashir Saheb to go right upto Moscow. What more favour can there be?"

"But Abba!" Ullug hesitantly said.

"Abba! How the people in big city are getting dressed up? I do not even have enough clothes."

"My son! At the moment get two pairs of clothes stitched. I have got some savings."

"But Abba! What about you . . . .?"

"Look Ullug! You cannot afford to miss such a chance.

"My work will go on. I will give you some money. Just find out what type of clothes are worn by students there and take two pairs of clothes or get them stitched ".

"Abba! I will send you some money from the amount saved from money that I will get for my food and provisions and I will come to meet you during holidays."

"Look my son! You will need money for your maintenance. Money is not to be wasted. But I am giving you one advice. Believe in what this old man is telling. Holy Book of Koran has said, "Never to be close to anyone. Keep away from wine, liquor and women. You are young but have a restraint. Holy Book of Koran teaches that. The biggest advice Holy Book of Koran is be away from fighting and quarrels ".

"From the destructive war of Mecca / Madina how much disturbed was Prophet Mohammed that you have read. Keep away from fights, quarrels or disputes, and, forgive them if they do something or do something that cause worry. Do you follow my son what I am saying?"

And the day of Ullug's leaving for Moscow arrived. Before the train started Alnashir said.

"Ismail Beg! Do not worry! Ullug is now on the road of success."

Ismail beg embraced his son and said "My son! Go and get all success in life."

Ullug never imagined the kind of "success" he will have in his journey of life.

CHAPTER 3

Human nature is to dream. color the dreams like a rainbow and try to shape them.

A youthful mind is so ambitious that with all wonderful desires and emotions it tries to attain the height of sky, sometimes want to reach the sky itself.

Ullug, for the first time in his life sat in a train and that also in first class.

Ullug was sitting in a first class compartment of a train. Alnashir and his wife-Begum were in next ca bin. Having two berths in the compartment, on second berth there was another passenger in Ullug's cabin. From his attire, he appeared to be a Russian. His face was extremely fair and thick red like a tomato and he was stocky,short and strong looking.His eyes though sharp but looked cruel. HIs face was without any emotion.He took out a pa d and a pen from his bag and faced Ullug.

.Ullug read his name, Muravaski, K.G.B. Ullug started thinking, What is it? In Russia and Soviet Union, KGB is a spy organization. In small a province like Uzbekistan still the fright of KGB was not felt. But he remembered the advice given by his father. As far as possible, avoid talking to unknown people. The spying agency of Soviet Union is very dangerous. It does not get moved by laws and bye laws of Moscow University. Alnashir Sir while boarding the train said "Govt. keeps an eye on every thing and everyone."

"Ullug! There will be another passenger in your cabin. If you find any difficulty call me immediately. Here everyone is under government's surveillance."

"What is your name?" Ullug got startled. Effortlessly he said "Ullug Beg."

"What place you belong to? Where are you going? Why are you going?

With an assault of so many questions at one time from a stranger, Ullug got cautious. In return he asked "What is your name? Where are you going? What are you doing?

Muravaski was watching Ullug with sharp eyes but was taken aback. "Do you know with whom are you talking?" Saying this he pointed his finger to the word KGB.

"No Sir! That's why I asked your name and your work." Ullug replied politely.

"That means you do not know what is KGB, isn't it so?"

"You stay in Tashkent, there is an atmosphere of war. We have to prepare a report on everyone. We have to be careful that no spy enters in our country. At present the war is on. You are aware of it, isn't it?

"Yes Sir! But I am not a spy, my motherland is Uzbekistan. I am a student."

"America and Islami countries are helping Afghanistan. Soviet Union has also sent its army. Do you know that?"

"Yes Sir!"

At that time

Alnashir came in Ullug's cabin, and saw that an interrogation of Ullug is being conducted. Seeing that he understood the seriousness, he told an entire story to Muravaski. He had a smile on his face when he heard the name of Dr. Khoshev.

"Now it is OK! I was worried about a spy. I am glad to know that he is going to Moscow for further studies. "Congrats" saying this he extended his hand towards Ullug for a shake hand. He took Muravaski's hand in his hand and felt as if he has held a fireball.

"Murawaski is hot blooded, he thought and Somewhere he had read that the blood of Chimpanzees is the hottest in the whole world. This man seems to be his descendant." A faint smile came to Ullug's face.

"You look really handsome when you are smiling. You are young, attractive and also appears to be brilliant. But be careful in Moscow. Be aware with foreign students. Many students are working as spy. Specifically give special attention to American students and American journalists ".

There after during the entire journey, he kept on talking about Soviet Union, about Russia and its Communist government, about KGB and explained the rules and role of KGB in detail, as if he was doing Ullug's brain wash and denudation of his thoughts.

Train arrived at Moscow's Central Station. For the first time Ullug saw so many people running around., as if they were not bothered about anybody.

Where is Tashkent and where is Moscow?. Catching the taxi, along with Alnashir and his wife, they reached at Dr. Khoshev's residence. Dr. Khoshev was in an emergency meeting, a conference with delegates from Africa. As they reached, at his home, Dr. Khoshev came there. He embraced Alnashir.

"Khoshev! this is Ullug" Dr. Khoshev kept on looking at Ullug. He looked at him from head to toe. A fair look, six feet height, dreamful eyes and a shine of brilliance on his face were liked by Dr. Khoshev.

Staying with him that night, next morning they all went to the college and its dormitory. After getting the registration done and leaving Ullug in a dormitory he said. "You also have to come to attend the wedding, understand?" and he gave him the address and telephone number. All these things took place in the dormitory, his room companion was also there, Dr. Khoshev's attention was drawn at him.

"What is your name? Where are you from?"

"Osman is my name! I am from Tazikistan. I have come here for further studies". Dr. Khoshev looked at him for two minutes. He could see the boiling lava in his eyes. He turned to Ullug said "Come Ullug! Leave me upto my car."

While walking towards the car he asked "Ullug! Do you know anything about Al-qaeda. About Saudi Arabia?"

"No Sir! Why?"

"Recently name of Osama Bin Laden is being discussed quite often. You may not be knowing that. Originally he is from Saudi Arabia. He wanted to bring all Islamic countries under one umbrella. He and his men are infiltrating Afghanistan and neighboring countries.

Have you seen the eyes of your room mate, your co-student? Seeing his eyes I am afraid. You are still new and kind hearted. Do not fall prey to his talks."

Saying this, Dr. Khoshev went away, but Ullug' got confused. He came back to his room.

He gave a smile to Osman. College was to start from next day. Both of them became friendly. Osman said. "You are well acquainted with Dr. Khoshev. He is the man who is helpful." Osman was between 20 and 22 years of age. Ullug felt that he was a selfish person. He has definitely come here with some motive. Thinking this, he became more cautious and decided to talk as less as possible. It was the time to pray, Ullug took out carpet. He remembered his father and set to write a letter to him. Osman was seeing all this. Ullug completed the letter and asked Osman "You do not want to write a letter?"

There was a burning fire in his eyes. Very next moment on getting control he became sad.

"No Ullug! I am now an orphan. During American bombarding in our small village on the border of Afghanistan, my family members lost their lives as a bomb fell on them. My Daddy, Father, Mother, brother and sister all died. I had gone out of the house so I survived. Before that I got an admission, so I came here."

"In your voice I felt lot of anger."

"Yes Ullug! I have got total hatred towards America. I will definitely take revenge on the country which totally destroyed my family."

Ullug seeing the lava of anger in Osman's voice and eyes Ullug was stunned. He decided "After completing my studies I will go back to my father".

'man proposes, God disposes.

No body knows what is written in one's destiny. Ullug did not know what is there in store for his life.

But how an ordinary human being can know what is destined for him?

The college semester started. Study syllabus started. Ullug started paying attention to his studies with all sincerity. He saw that unlike Tashkent in Moscow, boys and girls were sitting together, sitting on the same bench. So he had to change his dress code. He had to remove his Pathani dress and started wearing pant and shirt like other boys. His hair style was also changed. According to his religion, he had to keep beard and mustache, but he started trimming them and so, his face became more attractive. Still he was getting very hesitated feeling shy in talking with girls. But Russian girls were not fastidious. They were modern. He came into a new world seeing girls wearing full dress and short skirts. In his native place, as per Islamic religion women were still wearing veils-Burkha. He got a touch of modernization. Here he has to speak Russian language in place of Pukhtu or Uzbeki languages. In a dominion country like Uzbekistan, as per Russian law to learn Russian language was a must. So he had learnt the same. But there was no importance of English. Russian language was mandatory. Though everybody learned an English language.

One day he asked Dr. Khoshev "Sir! Is there any facility here to learn English language?"

Dr. Khoshev looked at his bright face. Ullug. had proved in his studies. He has proved his cleverness. He passed with merits in chemistry and biology. In research center, he was learning research work with perseverance. There also, he had additional interest in biology and botany. He was taking keen interest in different types of chemical and liquid substances.

"Ullug! Why? Why are you interested to learn English?

"Sir! English language is spoken in the whole world. If any time one has to go to foreign country for a conference, then how long one can depend on an interpreter?"

"Right from now you have started thinking about a conference?"

"Sir! I have an intense desire. I am hearing a lot of talks about chemical and biological warfare. Atomic weapons being highly destructive, no one can dare to take up war based on that. But do you think that on these two subjects anything can happen? Such like allegations are being made towards Sadaam Hussain. Isn't it?

"That means you are getting acquainted with politics and diplomacy am I right? But but be careful, never discuss your ideas and plans with anybody over here. I will get arrangements done for your study of English language. It will be useful to you. But Ullug! May I ask you one question? You talked about foreign country. Suppose for research work if you have to go to a country like Africa for research then would you go?"

"Sir! If English language is spoken in those countries, and, if it is beneficial to our Research Center, I will definitely go."

An ambition glowed in his eyes. "Ok! then be prepared for night classes."

In next two years, Ullug had almost got a mastery in English language. He used to inform his father about his progress. Four years got over. Since last two years he started getting salary from the Research Center. Ullug had never dreamt that he will start earning so early and that too so much. When he sent money to his father, he wrote "Abba! Allah has favored us. Now you have to leave your work. Dr. Khoshev sir is giving full attention to my studies and my salary is quite good. One more good news, that I have to go for a month to Zaire in Africa and Gombe Park located on the border of Tanzania to do research on Chimpanzees. Before going there I will come and see you."

Ismail Beg could not recognize a young man standing before him in shirt and pant. When that young man got down from the train, he saw that his father's puzzled eyes were searching for him. He ran saying "Abba!" He embraced him then only Ismail could realize that he was his son Ullug! Keeping him little away, he kept on seeing to his young and handsome son with satisfaction and praiseworthy look. Which father will not be proud seeing the progress of a promising son?

They came home and set, Ullug realized that from the money he is sending, it is enough only for maintenance. Next day he went out and brought masons and a contractor and made the roof of his house strong with roofing tiles. He got walls painted. He also bought one small sofa, a writing table, comfortable cots, quilts and new mattresses. Ismail got emotionally moved seeing his son's contrivance. He had never seen such luxuries in his life. His eyes became wet. Thinking that his later life will be quite comfortable and for that he kept on thanking God the Almighty.-Allah.

Ullug when went to the town and could see that Russian army with lot of enthusiasm proceeded from Tashkent to Caliph. Slowly Russia conquered Afghanistan! Najibulla's puppet government came in power. America got startled as it could not afford Russian supremacy on Afghanistan, Americans helped Mujahuddins to do guerilla war fare

When ullug returned asked his father,.

"Abba! Due to this, is there any there any problem on this side of Tashkent?"

"No! my son! But the subservient of our country bothers the politicians, Opposition parties sometimes raise their voice against the rule of Soviet Union over here, it is crushed. i We do not know when we will be independent. Moreover, Afghanistan being conquered, war centers have been opened in Tashkent and Caliph, so there is a strict control of soldiers."

"Abba! Please be careful, do not come in conflict with anyone. Do not go out alone until necessary."

"My son! You told me that you are going to Africa, a dark continent. I am worried about you."

"Abba! It is no more a dark country, Zaire is now independent from Government of France and Belgium, Tanzania became independent in 1961 from British Rule. All these countries are on the road of development. I am going there just for one month."

"Are you going alone or is there any body else with you?"

"Abba! We are a group of five. Dr. Khoshev is also with us. Nothing to worry, Now let me meet Mr. Alnashir, I have to go to moscow tomorrow."

After meeting Alnashir, Ullug took a seat in Tashkent train for Moscow. There were few soldiers in a train. And he got hesitant when he entered his cabin.

"Oh!" He exclaimed.

The man sitting on the opposite berth looked up. But did not recognize Ullug.

"You! You! Are Mr. Murawaski isn't it?" Impatiently Ullug asked.

"Yes! But how do you know me?"

"We have met twice before, First time when I was going to Moscow for further studies and second time in College dormitory. "Do you remember?"

"Oh! Are you Mr. Beg isn't it? you have changed a lot."

"Sir! time passes. Four years have passed away".

"Then Moscow has changed you."

"One should keep up with with time."

"You have become quite clever and smart."

"Sir! This is all due to education. But Sir! May I ask you one question? You took away one of the students from dormitory. What happened to him?"

Muravski looked to Ullug with a stare and said. "Whatever happens to an American spy, happened to him."

"That means."

"Punishment to a spy is death sentence."

"But was he really a spy?"

"When k.g.b. doubts any body, means he is a spy." Ullug shivered.

On reaching Moscow, within a week, under the leadership of Dr. Khoshev, Ullug and four other associates left for Nairobi in Soviet Union's official airline. 'Aero float'. Nairobi was an International Airport of Kenya. To go to other African countries, flights needed to be changed there. They landed at Kigoma situated on Tanganyika lake at Tanzania Zaire border. Gombe Reserve Park was on the Northern side. From there the journey started in a Jeep. Mr. kumezi came to receive them and head of the main research department of Gombe Park Mr. Mobilu also came there. A joint meeting was held. Dr. Khoshev and his delegates were given a place to stay in a modern lodge.

Ullug when he entered the hotel and went to his room, was enchanted to see the natural beauty of Africa being seen from his room window. Hotel was built on the bank of Lake Tanganyika providing each room a panoramic view of outside natural beauty. The length of lake Tanganika is almost the biggest of all the lakes of the world. The whole lake was like a small sea. This lake was on a border of Tanzania and Zaire. It was found by a roaming historian Mr. Livingstone. Kigoma town was looking beautiful on the bank of the lake. All types of people, such as Africans, Asians, Europeans and Arabs were staying here. Little away from Kigoma, there was Gombe Reserve Park, which was famous for Chimpanzees. It was quite surprising that Miss Goodall, a lady, found out that Chimpanzees reside in thick forests. She had a strange attraction towards these animals and she gave her whole life in looking after them. She wrote an internationally famous book on their minutest characteristics, way of their living and their method of reproduction. Because of that, the research personnel of the world got assembled here. Only after coming here, they came to know that Chimpanzees have fallen prey to one typical disease and to treat them was a problem. On one side it is African country, moreover this was quite an internal part. Even the human beings were not getting adequate treatment, while here it was the case of monkeys. There were two races of Chimpanzees, Kolobus and Rapio Anubis. Both the races were staying peacefully. But quite a few of them were infected by one incurable disease. These researchers have come to find out the clue. In the evening everybody assembled in the lounge of that hotel. Many were knowing Dr. Khoshev.

"Oh! Dr. Wellingdon nice to see you?" He was from england. Dr. Khoshev got up from his seat and greeted him.

"This is Ullug. He is a bright researcher. He has come with me. He is keenly interested in the diseases of Chimpanzees."

Next day all went to the park, Mr. Kumezi was with them. Few sick Chimpanzees were kept in a separate cage.

Dr. Smith of this park also came and said. "These Chimpanzees are suffering from Flu like symptoms. Due to that, his family members, his wife and two children are also got afflicted. Signs and symptoms of this disease are that first they get fever, coughing starts, has a running nose and headaches. There after they had nausea, vomiting and loose motion. As a result they start getting dehydrated and a need arises to give them drips. Medical facility over here is very low.

It takes a lot of time to reach medical aid here from Nairobi or Dar-e-Salaam. We do call medicines from

Zaire. But that country also has a lot of problems. All Chimpanzees blood has been sent for blood test."

"Sir! You say it's flu. What has been found in their reports?"

"We are just waiting for reports. We have already started giving medicines empirically started with fluids and antibiotics. Today is the third day. Prognosis is very poor."

"What about others who are in a cage this side . . . .?"

"Yes! In all other Chimpanzees who are the parents or brothers and sisters of those Chimpanzees, two are under the influence of flu and two others have stomach flu which means fever, shivering, cold, vomiting and loose motion. All of them are on a drip. But no one is showing signs of improvement. Today is the third day."

"Sir! Despite of giving I.V. drips and antibiotics, if there is no improvement then will there be any viral infection? Ullug's question alerted all others."

"Very good! Young man! We will see that also once the blood reports are received.

At that time Dr. Khoshev, his team and Dr. Willingdon were only there. Reports were received and Mr. Smith said" Mr. Beg! You are right. This is viral infection, other virus such as C.M.V., E.B.V. are negative. But what is this Ebola Virus?"

"Sir! I am aware of that virus." Ullug said. "It is highly destructive dangerous killer virus. Mainly it has a breeding in Zaire, Sudan, Ivory Coast, Northern Uganda and rain forests of West Pacific countries. The virus on this side is highly destructive and dangerous."

"But the whole family?"

"Yes! This virus is also like H.I.V. and getting spread due to blood, saliva, or secretion of any liquid from the body. Blood coming out of any cut, or by the secretion while kissing on lips or by intercourse or blood transfusion through the needle of a syringe. This virus incubets between 2 days to 21 days time, but as per available statistics in some cases an affected person or animal meets his death even in 3 days."

Everyone looked at Ullug with an appreciation. In the night, Dr. Khoshev called Ullug in his room when he was alone.

"Ullug! When did you do this extensive research?"

"Sir! When you told me about going to Africa from that very day I started this research. But I did not have a slightest idea that this virus will be found here."

"Hum!" saying this Dr. Khoshev was in deep thoughts, he was doing some calculations in his mind. Suddenly he said.

"Ullug! How does this virus get spread?"

"Sir! The spread becomes very fast if a needle of a syringe is injected from virus affected blood or if any one comes in contact with the patient of this disease."

"Ullug! Can I fully trust you?"

"Of course.?"

"Suppose we use this virus on humans . . . .?"

"Ullug got panicked," No! No! Sir! This is a very deadly virus. More destructive then an Atom Bomb. How can it be used on mankind? It is an extreme cruelty. God will not forgive."

"Look Ullug! Don't be emotional. Many countries are making use of atomic weapons for their self defense. Are they not aware of their destructive strength? To ensure that such weapons are not misused, some countries have entered into and signed joint agreements on this accord."

"You have heard that Sadaam Hussain is collecting chemical weapons. How will it be if we take the blood of the Chimpanzees as sample with us to make such biological weapons from these dying animals blood?"

Ullug got almost frozen hearing the proposal. He was aware of cruelty of KGB and Soviet Union. If he says 'No' then he may be murdered on the evidence that he has come to know about Dr. Khoshev's plans. Being helpless he had to give his consent.

In the night, both of them silently went to a dying Chimpanzees. He was used to get his blood checked. After seeing the needle, Chimpanzee extended his hand. With full caution and covering his head with apron and gloves, Ullug filled the full syringes with Chimpanzees blood, sealed the syringes, and kept the same in a small cylinder.

He helplessly gave the syringes in Dr. Khoshev's hands, Dr. Khoshev kept the cylinder in an ice-box. Dr. Wellingdon did not even know of it.

After a week, completing the research, conducting the seminars, writing in detail about Ebola Virus, every one went back with detailed information to their native place.

On reaching Moscow, Dr. Khoshev called Ullug in his office, seeing there Mr. Muravaski and a minister from Research Dept. of Soviet Government, Ullug got shivers.

"Ullug! Saying this he introduced both of them to him "These people have come here to praise your expertise, to appreciate your efforts. Now you are appointed as chief assistant in our research dept. And the virus which have brought along with us has been locked in the fridge of State Research Dept. This is minister Mr. Molokov ".

Then he turned to Mr. Muravaski and Mr. Molokov and said "Sir! There is nothing to worry for Ullug! His work is over here, and, he is going back to Tashkent. If you need you can contact him."

"It would be better if we have no need for the same. Isn't it Mr. Beg? We know each other quite well." Ullug was not that idiot not to understand the concealed meaning. He prayed to the God that there may not be any meeting with these people in future ever.

In few days, saying good bye to Dr. Khoshev, he started to go back to Tashkent to plan about his future. He became emotional remembering his father. He remembered the words of Dr. Khoshev "Ullug the help that you have done to the Soviet Union has been appreciated by President Brezhnev and he has sanctioned a life time pension for you." Remembering these words he became overwhelmed with this kindness by Dr. Khoshev.

After how many years he will meet his father? He became immensely happy. Instead of six years, he was returning after eight years. Seeing his father on the station, he jumped from the coach and embraced him. Seeing the strong and successful son, Ismail Beg looked to his son with all pride. On way to home in a taxi with his father, Ullug was giving detailed information to his father of his stay in Africa. Ismail told "my son! Now stay with me with peace and think about getting married. Now I am an old person.

"Oh Abba! Real happiness has come now. How can you go away like this? Don't you want to play with your grand child?"

Ismail Beg felt happy thinking about his son's marriage and said "My son! Are you aware of the order released by President Brezhnev? In the month of May

1988, i.e. after four months Russian army will be withdrawn from Afghanistan."

"Yes Abba! I have not to worry about a job. I am going to get pension.

"But my son! Political parties of Uzbekistan are pressing hard for independence from Soviet Union. If we become independent what will happen to your pension?"

"Abba! If one door is closed, God opens many more doors for us. Please do not worry. Now I want to stay with you only. I want to have my own family and live as an independent citizen in our independent country." Saying this Ullug embraced Ismail Beg.

But . . . But . . . how hollow it sounded., dreams . . . . have dreams ever became true?

CHAPTER 4

"Any problems?" seeing his unease Ismail Beg asked Ullug.

Ullug was getting restless without work.

He was getting pension regularly every month. So he was comfortable. But he was a research expert! How long can he keep on sitting like this without any work? In comparison to Tashkent, Moscow was quite modern. Moscow had inter regional population from different regions and religions. Communism did not have soft corner for religion, but Uzbekistan and its colonies, were followers of Islam. They all were staunch followers of Islam and were orthodox for any change. After Ullug's coming to Tashkent, people were looking strangely at him., disliking look at him for his dress. Helplessly once again he had to wear traditional dress.

Sitting on the river bank of Tashkent he was watching different avtivities of soldiers. By order of President Brezhnev, from May 1988 onwards Russian Army was being withdrawn. Najibulla's Puppet Government was formed in Afghanistan. Russian Officers were taking care of everything. Against Russian rule, Americans started giving military training to Mujahuddins giving them economic and military help. Activities to bring end of Puppet Govt. already started.

In a way, Pakistan was under a great influence of America. They started giving shelter to Mujahuddins. Moreover to see that troops with war material reach Kabul; Muslims of 'Radical Sunni Islamic Movement' were ready to ensure that such troops reach Kabul. At any cost Puppet Govt. was to be thrown out of Afghanistan, and they got an opportunity. In Soviet Union, President Gorbachev replaced President Brezhnev. New President was believing in liberalization. By February 1989, Russian Army was completely withdrawn from Afghanistan.

And Civil War broke out in Afghanistan.

In the meantime, Muslims of 'Radical Sunni Islamic Movement' adopted name of Taliban and while ensuring that war material reach to Kabul, they took the control on the border of Afghanistan. Najibulla tried to overcome that attack with the help of Russian Govt. But at that time, Talibans had support of America and Pakistan. While it was taking time for Russian goods to reach Afghanistan through hilly tracks of mountains, American material used to reach Afghanistan faster through Arabian Sea and the Karachi Port. Civil War lasted between 1989 and 1992, one million Afghanis were killed.

But effect of this movement was felt in Uzbekistan and nearby small countries where independence movement was in forefront. Political party of Uzbekistan took advantage of Gorbachev's liberalization policy and in 1991, Uzbekistan became independent. Movement of breaking Soviet Union started.

Uzbekistan became independent and with that event. Ismail Beg's fear came true. Ullug's pension was stopped Chechanya, Ukraine, Kazakistan, Kirgizstan, Tajikistan and other colonies sprang up as new nations. Major portion of Soviet Union became Russia.

Ullug started worrying as his pension was stopped. But as the luck would have it, Najibulla Govt. wanted to see Afghanistan as a developed country. While talking with Russian Officers it was decided to start one University at Kabul and it was also planned to start one modern Research Center in that University. Russian Officers were knowing Dr. Khoshev who recommended the name of Ullug as head of that centre.

Tired and desperate Ullug entered the house in a confused state of mind. His father was aware of his concern. He always used to give him a solace encouraging him and was telling him to keep faith in God.

"My Son! Why are you getting discouraged? Some one can snatch a loaf from your hand, but, not from your luck. You are intelligent. There is no other thing as safe as that, so do not lose courage."

At that moment a postman came. He gave one envelope in Ullug's hands. On envelope there was a stamp of Afghanistan Govt. Ullug got surprised. He opened the envelope and read "Mr. Ullug Beg! You have been appointed as head of Research Center of new University at Kabul. It is Dr. Khoshev's recommendation that you develop this Research Center". And there were other details of salary, rent and other related perks.

"Ullug! If you are accepting this appointment please let us know immediately"."

"Abba! I have got a job in Kabul." and he read the whole letter to his father. While reading the letter he thought that now he can do something by himself and that idea encouraged him.

"My Son! I was telling you to keep faith in God Almighty—Allah. How will be the atmosphere over there? This war and Mujahuddin's attacks and what not?"

"Abba! So long as Afghanistan has Russian support, till then there is nothing to worry. Perhaps if new govt. comes in power, even then what difference it makes? I am going to work for the govt whosoever will be in power. And Abba! Just think I will be head of the Research Center. Finally my ambition to do research work will be fulfilled."

"Allah! May give you all success. Kabul is closer than Moscow. I will occasionally keep on coming there. It is a great relief to me. My son! Now you should start thinking seriously about your marriage. Now . . . . !"

"Abba! Do not think like that. as you are my strength. Allah permits it will also be fulfilled."

While bidding farewell to Ullug, Ismail Beg was thinking "Where a human life takes a turn?"

With a new zeal, Ullug took charge of the Research Center. He started his work with all sincerity. He made his center quite famous with his expertise. Very often he was thinking of the virus he found in Africa. Now Soviet Union is divided so that virus will be in possession of Russian Govt.

He started corresponding with Dr. Khoshev through his government. In the beginning there were few suggestions, but no mention about Ebola Virus. And after some time the correspondence stopped on Dr. khoshev' front.

One day in an University function a Russian Officer came. Ullug asked him "Mr. Laddimar! Any news from

Dr. Khoshev? We need his guidance and suggestions in matter of one research.

"Oh! Mr Beg! Don't you know? Before three months he is killed in a car accident."

Ullug knew that regarding Ebola Virus, KGB Director Muravaski, Dr. Khoshev and he only three persons knew. To ensure that Dr. khoshev may not be a problem for the govt, he might have been removed from the scene. But now communism was out of Russia. Corruption and power of Mafias were very much seen due to liberalization policy. Then whether mafia coming to know about Dr. Khoshev, have they removed him.?

Ullug while sitting in his office was thinking about this. As he was in Kabul, he was away from Mafias and so had a relief. In the meantime his office door got knocked, "May I come in?"

"Please come."

Holding a lab test tube in one hand, a beautiful lady came in. Even now ladies in Afghanistan were wrapping scarf on their heads and only keeping their face open. But the beauty of that lady who came in was not remaining concealed. Really speaking education in ladies was very much less. Only few ladies were making progress that too in small proportions. Farhana being daughter of the head of a Govt. Dept. she got an opportunity to be educated. She was working in a research department lab. She was very bright. She picked up almost all the work of Mr. Ullug.

"Sir! I have come to show you this result."

"Which result! Farhana?" Ullug seeing Farhana was getting soft. He liked this young lady at first sight. While working together, he was attracted to her but could not say anything.

"Sir! The result is of the test we are conducting on new Virus found by us."

"Any success?"

"Sir! Something is missing which needs to be located. But one question is confusing me."

"What is that?"

"While testing, some liquid fell on the table. Immediately table top got burnt. If this liquid falls on our skin then will it have an acidic effect?"

Ullug got up from the chair.

"Farhana! Have you told this thing to anyone else?"

"No Sir! I came to you the very moment result was known."

"Farhana! Continue testing. But no one should come to know about it.It may be misused. Keeping in mind an unbalanced political conditions over here, we have to be careful."

"Yes Sir! You are right. But Sir! a Young man who is recently appointed keeps on asking me questions."

"Do not worry Farhana! I will take care."

"Thank you Sir!"

"Farhana! is it necessary you should call me Sir?" Ullug abruptly asked.

"Sir! How is it possible?"

"Farhana! Don't you understand why I am saying so". She blushed and Farhana left the room.

Ullug felt happy. He thought of calling to his father. Finally, he could see his hope getting fulfilled.

Four years passed of Research Center being established started getting name and fame all over.

Afghanistan's political structure and infra structure had collapsed due to civil war, American attacks from Pakistan border and movement of Taliban's Radical Muslims were on increase, military goods were being transported as commercial goods in trade caravans.

Their terror fear was on increase in border villages. All of a sudden in one big attack, Kabul was under a siege. In 1996, Najibulla's Govt. was on the way of collapsing and finally it collapsed. Talibanis became masters of Afghanistan. Najibulla ran away and along with him, Russians fled. They were totally worn and torn while they were fleeing away through hilly areas. America was celebrating it's victory.

Initialy American soldiers were moving in the streets of Kabul, Taliban took out a Mandate that women have to look after their homes, and family only. They have not to go to the schools for study, Maderesas (School for children) were opened. All ladies have to put on masks-Burkhas. It was becoming difficult for women to protect their woman hood.

Ismail Beg kept on looking at Farhana and her beauty. Ullug invited Farhana's father also at his home. With everyone's consent, engagement ceremony took place. Farhana had to leave her job due to Mandate of Taliban Govt.

"Ullug! my son!" Ismail said after guests left and when both were sitting alone." Finally Allah heard my plea. I will get peace of mind once you get married."

"Abba! That moment is not far away."

"My son! When can I return to Tashkent? I will come back on your marriage."

"No! Abba! Now you have to stay with me."

"What about our house?"

"It will be taken care of. You stay here coolly."

"My Son! This new Govt.? Any danger? These American Soldiers?"

"The country and the University needs Research Center. We have nothing to be afraid of."

"OK! My son! Allah may give you all the progress."

"I am indeed grateful to Allah for your getting such a beautiful wife. OK! It's my time for doing prayers."

Foreseeing beautiful dreams of future, Ismail Beg spread his hand on a woven carpet kept on the ground.

Are the dreams of anyone are ever fulfilled?

CHAPTER 5

"Mr. Ambassador! I have few urgent matters to be discussed with you. Thanks for giving me time."

Mr. Moynihaan! You are American Army colonel at Afghanistan. Something important must have come up! Tell me what is all that?"

"Mr. Berrymur! Do you trust these Talibanis?"

"There is no question of trusting them, they need us to protect their established interest in this country. They have to depend on us for money, arms and ammunitions".

"Do you believe that Mr. Omar, head of Talibanis will not be getting help of money and arms from other places?"

"Mr. Berrymur got alert and said. "Is there any purpose for you to think like this? Do you have any important information?

"Sir! Pakistan is on our side. But Taliban has come out with a mandate. It expresses Islamic conditions."

"All of them are Muslims. Islam is their religion. What is unfair in that?.

"Are other Islamic countries not helping them?"

"Mr. Moynihaan! To drive out Russia, We, Pakistan and other Islamic countries, such as Saudi Arabia, Iraq give them support is quite fair."

"Sir! When the reference of Saudi Arabia is made, I am informing you that one call received from Saudi Arabia was intercepted. It is a startling matter so we have to be alert."

"What do you say?"

"a phone call came on Osama Bin Laden of Muslim Association saying that if Osama is here in Afghanistan, then, where the ammunitions are to be sent? Moreover, Osama had a talk with Mr. Omar and the topic was that American army should go away from here.

"Hum! What do you think in this matter?"

"We may have to move out any time from this country but information about Al-Qaeda which FBI has acquired is quite alarming."

"Why?"

"Osama Bin Laden's attitude is anti America. He has total hatred for America. Making an association of all Muslim countries he wants to pressurize America. He cannot fight with us on one to one basis, so he wants to take the support of terrorists. He has been exhiled from Saudi Arabia under America pressure, for which he wants to take its revenge on America.

"How?"

"He is assembling muslims and Guerilla camps have been opened in the mountain caves of Karakoram and Khyber ghat."

"He has started training young and unemployed Muslims."

"Suicide Bombers are trained, which will cause a problem for us."

"I will discuss all these issues in a meeting with Mr. Omar. Please keep me informed about developments here."

"Sir! One more thing. Taliban has got a start in Pakistan. Even today quite a few of them are in Pakistan. They have opened two / four associations and most of them have camped in Swat Valley. Pakistan govt. has given them free hand. They do not observe law of the land instead Talibanis are the rulers that is also a matter causing worry."

"ok! i will inform Mr.President about this. First let me talk to Mr. Omar"

"Mr. Omar!" Mr. Berrymur quietly proceeded the conversation. "Who is this Osama Bin Laden?"

Mr. Omar got startled. Then composed himself and he said. "He is a Muslim who has run away from Saudi Arabia."

"Has Afghanistan given him shelter?"

"Shelter! No! Any Muslim can come and stay in this country ".

"Their movements! Arms and Ammunitions, Guerilla Training? Knowing all these will America not get worried?"

"Why should you worry?"

"Still defense of this country is our responsibility."

"Someday you have to be out of this country isn't it? To take that responsibility we are becoming capable."

"Yes! But what will be the state of affairs that time? You have to see that such movements are stopped. It is in the interest of this country".

"Right! I know what is required to be done in the interest of this country. And Yes! Please direct American soldiers to be disciplined."

"Why? Do you have complaints?"

Yes! We have given a mandate to ladies not to go to schools and not to come out of their houses. For small children we have opened maderessas (schools) for children. Educated ladies will teach Holy Book of Koran to children. Please see that these ladies are not being harassed.

Mr. Berrymur came out from there. He was thinking "Talibanis themselves were harassing ladies and were blaming American soldiers." Slowly he was getting worried. He felt that today while talking Mr. Omar's behavior was strange. He was not polite and ready to fight by locking horns. He would not behave like this unless has acquired a strong support from elsewhere other than Americans.

"Dear Farhana! After working in a research lab, how do you feel going

to Maderessa to teach?" Farhana's influential father asked her.

"Abaa!, it is not the subject in which I feel interested. But now with the change in Govt. their rules are to be obeyed."

"But dear! You have to go all the way at the and of the city to the Maderessa which I feel is not right.

All over, there are Talibanis, and, movement of American soldiers, so please ensure that no untoward incident happens.

"Abaa! I have a permit issued by the govt. to move anywhere and to go to teach then why to worry?"

"Yes dear! But be cautious. What are the news of Ullug? I have not seen him for quite some time . . ."

"He came yesterday. You had gone to work. He is also very busy. Ok Abaa! It's time for me to go to Maderessa ".

Due to unstable atmosphere in Kabul, transport facility was almost nill. Farhana had to walk all the distance. Now she had to wear mask—burkha also. After removing the mask-burkha in Maderessa, she used to teach the students. There also quite a few Talibanis used to come to check whether everything is done according to their mandate or not. There was severe punishment for defaulter. Talibaan rule was full of fear and threat, while under supervision of U.S. soldiers harassment was much less.

Farhana used to go to Maderessa located at end of the city. On account of bombing, few buildings got dilapidated condition.

On the other side, American soldiers were taking care to see that there is no bombing from hilly area. Many of soldiers were quite young in age and on face they were looking quite safe. On being recruited in the army, they come at an unknown place, away from their family and the country. But what a human being is not doing in lure for money? Sometimes remembering home, sometimes members of the family, these young soldiers after duty hours were occasionally taking drinks. These young soldiers after completing, their duty while returning to their campus had to pass through Farhana's Maderessa. Two / Three soldiers were returning together. Farhana could see that one handsome young soldier was invariably standing there while passing through Maderessa and used to stare at Farhana through the window of her class room. On being aware, Farhana was putting on her mask-burkha.

Today it was already evening time in the school. Slowly guardians were taking away their children. Farhana could leave only after all the children had gone. After the last child left, Farhana came out of Maderessa. Roads were barren, nobody was nearby, so Farhana did not put on her mask-burkha. While passing through a dilapidated house, she saw that one American soldier was standing under a tree holding in one hand aluminium can of alcohol. He was sipping from that can., American soldiers being in this country people did not have a fright as much that for Talibanis.

Farhana came out without any suspicion. That American soldier went behind her. Farhana saw him. She gave a bit smile and walked further. But soldier misunderstood her smile.

He held her hand, and said, "Lady! I like you". There was a foul smell coming from his mouth. she took away her hand and increased her speed. That soldier also increased his speed. Coming near to the dilapidated building, she hid herself behind its wall. But the soldier did see her. He came very close to her. Farhana spoke in English. "Stay away from me, you are here to protect us."

But soldier was drunk and was not in his senses. He dragged Farhana holding her hand. Farhana could not match his strength. The soldier pulled her scarf which got stuck to her neck and holding the scarf from both the hands he pulled Farhana towards him. Her throat was getting choked and she had breathing trouble. She wanted to scream but she could not and slowly she was losing her consciousness. In few moments she became unconscious. The soldier was not aware of what was happening. Getting no protest, after raping her, he came out limping from the dilapidated house. In the meantime two other American soldiers came from opposite direction. They saw him. Coming near, they saw Farhana lying on the ground. They reached there running. One American soldier covered her naked body with his Jacket and her scarf. He kept his hand near her nose, and felt that there was no breathing. Both her lips were blue, the soldiers understood that she is dead. They slapped the rapist soldier. Later on he came to his senses and understood the seriousness. He started crying sobbingly, taking out Farhana's address from her purse, she was taken to her house.

Farhana's parents a got a rude shock. Ullug came to know about incident and he came running. He took her head in his lap. He started crying. After sometime he got up. Having come to know that this is the misdeed of an American soldier, firm determination was seen on his face. On next day he demanded justice.

On coming to know about the incident Mr. Omar sent a call for Mr. Moynihaan. Mr. Omar said "Mr. Moynihaan. for that soldier's misdeed you have to hand over him to us. He will be judged according to law of this country. He will be given a death sentence in open market place in presence of people".

Mr. Omar looked to Mr. Moynihaan with sharp eyes and then to Ullug. Mr. Moynihaan said,. "Mr. Omar he was our soldier and his court marshal will take place in U.S.A. So he has been deported to America for his punishment".

"It cannot happen that way,Ullug said," knowingly you have interfered in process of justice in this country." Seeing his blazing face Mr. Moynihaan and Mr. Omar got shivers, Mr. Omar coolly got up. He went to Ullug,

He kept his hand on Ullug's shoulder and turning to Moynihaan he said "You can go."

Seeing Ullug's blazing face Moynihaan got frightened.

"Mr. Ullug Beg! Please cool down. Whatever was to happen has happened, you have our total support. Your face reveals a deadly vengeance. You have got one option. How to retaliate for the misdeeds of an American? Isn't it?"

There was a cunning smile on Omar's face "Mr. Beg! You will get all financial help. Please be tactful."

And Ullug got up with one dangerous determination.

CHAPTER 6

Mr. Wellingdon did not even know that Dr. Khoshev and Mr. Ullug have already left for Moscow from Gombe Park. He woke up in morning and after getting fresh, he went for a stroll on the side where sick Chimpanzees were kept. He was pondering that why all these Chimpanzees have fallen ill and why could they not be treated and saved? If their blood, urine and stool cultures are examined, then it can be known that due to which virus or germs they are killed. Then their treatment can be initiated. In this forest area, there was no facility, even to get I.V. drips available. Whatever was in the lab had to be used very sparingly.

He approached near cages where they had gone yesterday and found a commotion there. Mr. Mobulu and Mr. Kumezi both were already there and were giving instructions. In border towns of Zaire and Tanzania, Kiswahili language was common.

"Upesi, Upesi, sana (quick, make it very quick) Huyu Zothe na Kuisa Kufwa (All of them are dead) Towa Huyu, Paleka Pande Ele. (take them out from the cages and take them to that side)."

In the meantime, on seeing that Mr. Wellingdon was coming, Kumezi went to him "Oh! Mr. Wellingdon thank God that you have come. Just now we got news that Dr. Khoshev and his companion had to go back back to Moscow from Nairobi for some urgent work."

"What has happened to these two Chimpanzees? Did they die all of a sudden?"

"Yes! Mr. Wellingdon! IT seems these viruses kill them just in three days, with fever cough, vomiting diarrhea."

"Mr. Kumezi! were their blood, urine and stool cultures got examined?.."

"Sir! Where do we get these facilities in this forest? All these things are needed to be sent to Kinshasha, the capital city of Zaire or Tanzanian capital Dar-es-Salaam, otherwise to Nairobi. If it is not possible there also then to London.

Mr. Wellingdon as if reflected his own thought said! "Listen! I have come here from London for a research in this matter. I have got all sterilized equipments. If you say so then samples blood, urine and stool of these animals I will take them to London, I will make self examination and send you a report."

Who will say no if all problems get solved by themselves?.

Mr. wellingdon went back to his room. He lifted Test Tube Kit Box and made his companion Rushdi ready to join him.

"Rushdi! We have to take blood samples of recently died Chimpanzees and also to take samples of blood, urine, stool and saliva of those who are alive. Please put on gloves, as virus\ bacteria can be fatal. Even the slightest touch or contact can be fatal, collect all samples with due care. They are to be examined in a lab once we reach London."

Rashdi got excited as his ambition is nearly fulfilled.

. His father was a Jeweler in Karachi-Pakistan. They have settled in St. Thomas Island in Caribbean sea. Many Indians have settled in Caribbean Island. The tourists were purchasing lot many ornaments made out of gold and diamond precious stones. So they became rich. Instead of sending Rushdi to America, he was sent to London for research work as he thought education in England is superior to any other country of the world. He had great fascination for research work and so he was sent to London from St. Thomas Island.

With due care, he collected all samples. Mr. Wellingdon was standing right in front of him. Recently Al-Qaeda and Talibani groups were quite powerful. Their terrorism was gradually increasing. The name of Muslims was taken with great care. As with bad elements, good elements have to suffer in same way good number of Muslims also had to suffer. Every Muslim was looked at with suspicion. So Rushdi was avoiding to be identified as a Muslim.

Mr. Wellingdon took all samples, properly packed them and while going to his room, he placed them in a small fridge and kept the same in a big safe. The safe was to be taken to London in an Aero plane. While keeping samples in a fridge, Mr. Wellingdon was thinking that Dr. Khoshev and his companion came here for research work, then why all of a sudden they went away? That too stealthily. If so why? Dr. Khoshev was internationally known in this field then why has he done like this?

He was not getting answers to these questions. He got busy for his next day's traveling schedule. While boarding the plane he told to Mr. Mobulu and Mr. Kumezi.

"On receiving the reports I will send same to you, and I will also convey which treatment is to be given. But both of you must see that you or your servants do not touch these Chimpanzees or their blood and saliva.

"Why Sir! Have the animals got an H.I.V.?

"No! Nothing is like that. Due to their contact if bacteria\virus will infect you, then it will not take time to spread amongst your relatives, friends, family members and in nearby communities."

"Why did you come to that conclusion." Have you noted that in how much time the infected Chimpanzee were found dead after infection?"

"No! We have not noted. But they died in two or three days period after getting infection."

"Then just think. If you are affected, then your family members, relatives, and friends can they remain safe? Moreover keep an eye on the researchers coming from all over the world. I have a doubt, that these viruses are dangerous. I will be sending the report very soon."

Rushdi was listening all this intently.

Leaving Mr. Mobulu and Mr. Kumezi in an astonishing situation, Mr. Wellingdon's aircraft left for London.

"Mr. Chandrashekhar Reddy."

Reading the name plate Miss. Zeba just stood there. She had a charming smile on her face. She knocked the door. Home land Security Research Lab was opened in this modern section. Chief of that section was Mr. Shekhar Reddy who was also known as Shekhar. He was appointed on two year's H.I Visa, Zeba had to meet him in connection with certain tests and results. Shekhar was always remaining extremely busy in his work. He had never seen Zeba, Shekhar was a native of a suburb of Karnataka, Andhra Pradesh border, In India. People from that area are moderately of fair skin. Shekhar was fair looking and well built. He had thick black ruffulled hair and he was wearing glasses,

, so he was looking like a professor. From the face he was looking of 30-32 years of age but his smile was very charming. Zeba had a liking for him. Many times for no reason, she used to come there just to see his smile. She used to make fun of him. A smile used to come on his face. To see that smile Zeba used to ask funny questions at times for no reason.

Under pressure of work, he was not in a position to understand the reason, but was praising her works ethics. Nothing was going unnoticed from Zeba's sharp eyes. Recently, terrorism was getting spread in India. There were lot of Muslims in Hyderabad, the capital city of Andhra Pradesh. So she used to make inquiries in that context. But Shekhar was serious. He could not think anything except research. He was not interested in unrelated topics. He was a good painter and artist. Recently he started making a new painting for his house.

Zeba many a times used to ask him "Which painting have you started recently?"

Seeing a sweet smile on his face Zeba was feeling happy. This innocent, charming learner type of youth was liked by Zeba. Moreover she was getting impressed on seeing his work abilities.

Listening a knock on the door Shekhar got up. He opened the door and saw Zeba standing there with a broad smile. Shekhar's voice got overwhelmed. "Come! Come! Miss Khalid". She took a letter kept inside the door. Shekhar got the point, with a charming smile he said. "I have forgotten to collect the letter. Zeba is it OK?"

"Hum! No! It is not OK! What is going on here?" Saying this Zeba came to Shekhar's desk and seeing sketches lying there she said.

"Oh my God! Why have you painted such small snakes?" Is there no work nowadays so that you are doing such funny paintings? Are you thinking of someone?" There was a smile Zeba's face.

"No Zeba! This is not painting. These are the images of Viral germs found from research results."

"Oh! My God? Are they like these? Are they magnified ones?" And she became serious.

"Shekhar! Is it the testing of tissues recently received from Africa?"

"Zeba! These are the pictures of viruses sent by Mr. Wellingdon from London. From his writings it is evident that on account of these deadly viruses any one can die immediately."

"Have you read anything about that virus?. Virus are of different types. From them all of us get fever. Flu can also be considered as Viral infection".

"Yes! But they believe that these viruses are fatal. His doubt proved correct. He had sent a report to our research director. But on the envelope he has mentioned. "Private" and so I do not know what is in that report?" Zeba was thinking something. In the meantime Research Director Mr. Patton came in.

"What is going on between two of you?" He said with a smiling face. He was quite a joyful person. He was kind hearted too. Perhaps Zeba's feelings for Shekhar he knew about.

"Sir! I came here to see Dr. Shekhar" said Zeba "He is a person worth being taken care of. Isn't it?" Zeba felt shy.

He took away envelope from Shekhar. He started to go away but he turned back and said.

"Dr. Shekhar! I feel let us read this letter here in your presence". Saying that he opened the letter and read loudly.

"Ebola" Zeba and the research director exchanged the looks with each other, as if something was conveyed "Was this then the reason for Zeba to come and meet Shekhar?"

Mr. Omar called Mr. Ullug. On receiving his call, dangerous thoughts were getting defused in Ullug's mind. Being composed he got ready to go.

There was a vacuum in Ullug's life on account of Farhana's death. Ismail Beg also had a big shock on Farhana's death. His dream was torn to pieces.

In recent times no proposal can be placed before Ullug for marriage. His behavior had also undergone a change. Loving, kind hearted, emotional Ullug, became rough and speechless. He was doing all the work like a machine. There was a difference also in his behavior with his father. Ismail Beg was aware of his mental condition. Keeping quiet he kept on thinking. Suddenly he started feeling that he is getting old. He was broken emotionally.

He had a strong belief that he is not going to survive for long. His dream to see Ullug's family life may remain incomplete. Doing prayers he was looking to the sky. Perhaps Allah may do some favor.

"Abba! I am going to meet Mr. Omar."

"My son!! May I tell you one thing? New Talibani laws will drive this country backwards and the country will be staunch and orthodox once again. Even otherwise Americans have received orders to leave this country. What can be the reason?"

Hearing the name of America, Ullug's face became furious, his hands were tightly clenched and he ground his teeth. He said. "Abba! Now our country does not need these tyrants. They have received the support from person like Osama Bin Laden.

"But why he is staying in mountains?"

"He is building Guerilla Camps. He is training Jihadi trainees. He wants to make all Muslim countries Islamic. He is a strong enemy of Western countries, more specifically of America. Under the cover of giving protection, these Americans have killed Afghanis and our Muslim brothers ".

"My son! You have to take care, you don't enter into politics. You have work with research and you have to do that only. Oh! I just remembered that you went with Dr. Khoshev to Africa. You brought some samples, have you received the reports?"

"Abba! Those samples are with Russian Govt. so it won't be available. I am working on some other research and for that I might have to go to London."

"There are many Muslims in London. Maderessas are also opened there to teach Koran. One Mr. Mullah Khushroo is staying there. He is from Tashkent. I know him. If you are going to London then make it a point to see him."

"OK! Abba."

Though the country was having total poverty sitting in his ultra modern office, Mr. Omar said "Come! Take a seat!"

Talibanis grabbed everything in their control like what outlaws do. There was an atmosphere of terror in common man. Everything was done at gun point.

Now tell me! Mr. Beg! How your research work is going on?"

"For want of adequate facilities it is so-so."

"How the country will be benefited by your research work?" Ullug got startled listening this question.

"We can make vaccines to stand against germs spreading diseases. We can protect children from meeting unnatural deaths."

"How the country's defense matters will be benefited by your research."

"Army is there to protect them ".

"Yes! But for that there is a need for arms and ammunition isn't it?

"That we can get from missionaries of Western countries and the agencies selling arms ".

"See! We have driven away Russia. It got divided. To get the help from there will be difficult ".

"Then other western country and Germany?."

"Arms can also be made available from Osama and Al-Qaeda organization. Now recently they are talking something different."

"What? Chemical and Biological Warfare to spread terrorism such chemicals and use of viruses is enough. No need to waste money for purchase of arms."

"But so far we have not reached that stage. There are no facilities in our lab for that kind of work. Finance is also required for development."

Mr. Omar clapped.

A well built person having beard and mustache, and wearing traditional dress and rifle on his shoulder came out of other room.

"Could you not recognize him?." There was confusion on Ullug's face.

"He is Mr. Osama Bin Laden."

Ullug got up from his chair, as if Aura of some non-auspicious object was around him. He kept on looking at Osama's face. He kept on seeing his face full of firm determination with piercing and cruel sparkling eyes. It was difficult to measure his depth, and as if in that depth, he wanted to submerge the whole world. Effortlessly he spoke "Walekum Salaam" (Greetings).

"Asalaam Malekum!" (Return Greetings) One serious destructive tone came out in his words.

"Both of you sit" said Omar.

Mr. Beg! This is Osama Bin Laden! He is prepared to help us in all matters. He has his own underworld organization. He is fully aware of world affairs." Saying this Mr. Omar turned to Osama. Osama understood his move. He kept his hand on Ullug's shoulder, Ullug felt as if he is crushed under a rock. One un likable magnetic substance was making him hypnotized.

"Mr. Beg! Did you go to Africa when you were a student?" Ullug was surprised, Osama's all powerfulness was making Ullug more nervous. "There you met Mr. Wellingdon. Isn't it?"

"You silently left from there with Dr. Khoshev. Two or Three days after you, Dr. Wellingdon also left for London taking all samples with him."

"Samples?" Ullug got surprise.

"Yes! those samples of Chimpanzees. Dr. Wellingdon must have shown you the report."

"What are those viruses? It must have been known that how those Chimpanzees died. If we know the details then we can spread Bio-Terrorism. Moreover against our enemy America, it can be priceless ammunition. Isn't it? What type of help can we expect from you against America—a common enemy of all of us."

Ullug wound opened.

"Do not worry for money or finance".

"You will get all facilities. Over there, there is one Mr. Rushdi, companion of Dr. Wellingdon. He will give you all details. Make preparation to go to London"

As if it was an order.

CHAPTER 7

After returning from a meeting with Mr. Omar, Ullug said, "Abba! I have to go to London".

"Why? Is there any specific reason? You met Mr. Omar to today isn't it? Your visit to London is in relation to that meeting?."

For the first time Ullug could not talk eye to eye with his father. Is it that he had to conceal something? People who are not in a position to face the truth and a justice both at the same time behave like this.

"No! Abba! I have to go on behalf of my Research Center. You were telling that one Mr. Khushroo is living there. Shall we ring him up? I do not know anyone over there."

"Yes! My son! He was my very good friend. We have not met for quite a long time but he has not forgotten me. You call him and tell him when will you reach there."

In the night he was thinking that, how could Rushdi and Osama Bin Laden met? Rushdi is a resident of St. Thomas Island which is a part of Caribbean Islands. He had gone to London for further studies. He came to Africa with Dr. wellingdon as his trusted companion. There he met Ullug. Ullug was confused but he realized that one thing was certain that Osama Bin Laden was a very shrewd person. He is getting information from all the corners of the world. After going to London, he should meet Rushdi first and Dr. Wellingdon there after. It is imperative to know what relations he has with Al-Qaeda.

After completing all preparations to leave, he rang up Mullah Khushroo from his office. "Salaam Alekum, Uncle! I am Ullug! Son of your friend Ismail Beg. I am calling from Kabul. In connection with my research work, there is a possibility of my coming to London and can i be your guest for few days?".

"Oh! My Son! Do you need to ask for that? Come with pleasure. Ismail also must have been aged like me isn't it? Have you got married? Someone is needed to look after domestic affairs. Not married? God will definitely find good companion for you." Saying Allah hafeez, he put down the phone. Ullug felt very comfortable from the warmth that he received from Mullah Khushroo. He started preparing for his London assignment.

Pakistan Airlines had a direct flight to London from Islamabad via Kabul. After finishing Airport formalities he took a seat in the plane. On adjoining seat there was a middle aged Muslim Lady. She looked like a Pakistani one! After putting on seat belt he leaned his head on back of his seat and started thinking. "Journey! How is the journey of life? Cannot be known, cannot be understood. Nobody knows where is the destination! Many a times, the destination is like a mirage which keeps on slipping, just as the sand slips from your hands, just as Farhana slipped away.

And the way in which Farhana was badly treated, remembering all that his anger arose. He was full of fury. His face was red with anger. In the meantime, he heard a sobbing from the next seat. He turned his face to a lady on next seat and saw that she was crying. In her hand, there was a photograph of a handsome young man. She wiped off her tears the moment Ullug looked at her, she said "He is my son Rahim".

"Why are you crying Aunty? Has something happened unwarranted.?"

"No! No! Nothing is like that as you think but still it is unwarranted."

"Please excuse me, I have no right to interfere in your personal matters. I have lost my mother and seeing you, I have a motherly feeling for you, that is why I am asking what happened to Rahim."

"We came to Karachi from London for three months and met Mr. Naqvi, head of Lashkar-e-Toyba and Mr. Rasul Khan of Al-Qaeda. It was a terrible moment. It is fine for young Muslims staying here. But even in London they mislead youngsters in name of Jihad, and do their brain wash. They train youngsters for suicide attacks. In Islamic religion there are no such destructive activities. Yes! One can take the training for self defense, but what do you get by killing innocent people? Moreover Jihad against whom? Our people?" Nobody has created a war like situation against our religion. My son was quite childish. He got in their trap and said to me."

"Mom! I have submitted myself to Lashkar-e-Toyba and Al-Qaeda. Now I will be fighting for Jihad."

"My son! Jihad against whom?"

"Against our enemies."

"Who are our enemies?"

"Britain and America."

"My son! English people have given you protection, then how can they be our enemy?"

"Mom! At present soldiers of those countries are in Afghanistan and Iraq. They are murdering our Muslim brothers."

"How can you call it a murder? It is a war. In war even British soldiers are getting killed."

"Mom! If they would not have started a war with us then so many Afghanis and Iraqi people would not have been killed."

"My son! think twice before being tools in hands of others, let our intellect not be maligned."

And he got himself recruited in that group. I wish we did not come here.

"Are you not proud for your son? He is prepared to fight for our religion, everyone has to revolt against injustice."

"My son! Firstly one has to understand the definition of word injustice. If any one or more people have done injustice to you, go and fight with such people. Is it fair that for such a reason you declare war against entire community.?"

Ullug remained silent. He was thinking, injustice to him has been made by an American soldier, then instead of punishing, him, is it fair to become a terrorist and punish all the Americans? He got confused, he had reason to be angry. Tears were in his eyes. Seeing a question in the eyes of co-passenger she started telling about her sufferings. So she said, "My Son! Prophet Mohammed has said that everyone has to pay for one's deeds. How do we know what were the deeds of Farhana in this birth or previous births?. Prophet Mohammed has written in Koran to forgive the misdeeds of every one. Forget about misdeeds of others. You seem to be clever, make use of that quality."

Listening to what she said, Ullug started thinking. But he was not in a position to control the anger arising in him. In the meantime, these was an announcement. "Plane landing in fifteen minutes on Heathrow Airport. Tighten your seat belts."

He composed himself and he got ready for. disembarking. After. customs and immigration formalities, Ullug came out. On opposite side of the exit gate some persons were standing holding placards to receive incoming passengers. Ullug read his name on one of such placards. He went there and along with the placard holder and he took a seat in a taxi.

The taxi driver looked like a Muslim. The picture of mecca was kept on dash board of that Taxi. Taxi started and Ullug asked the driver "What is your name?"

"Amir Khushroo."

"Maulana is your . . . .?"

"He is my daddy.-Abba He runs a Maderessa."

"And you are a taxi driver?"

"Yes! During Russia Afghanistan war daddy came here."

Ullug got surprised that where Mr. Khushroo and Abba met each other?

"In Maderessa people come to learn Koran. Isn't it? Will all the children be Muslims from London only?"

"Over and above from London children from refugees of other countries are also admitted here."

"Which side are we going?"

"This is suburb Slough. Daddy started his activities here. But now there are problems."

"What type of difficulties?"

"Due to color bar and racial enmity, refugees from Jamaica, Nigeria, Somalia and specially the youngsters have formed gangs and all here are afraid of them. Against this, English youngsters have also formed gangs and now they are armed with weapons. There is a fear of security, and my Daddy also has received threats."

"Then what will happen now?"

"Here suburb of Harrow is quite safe. Muslims also stay there. We have decided to shift on that side. We have got one nice house, Entrance is quite big. There, with the help of county administration Daddy is constructing one Maderessa. Look! We have reached!"

Amir looked like of 25 years of age. He had strong faith in religion. He had a lot of respect for his father.

Before entering in the house Ullug asked "Amir are you in a position to maintain your family?."

"ALLAH
is very kind to us."

"If I need, can you provide taxi service? With one condition that you have to take taxi fare."

Amir liked this young man and said to Ullug "Brother! You are just entering the house. Please come in, perhaps daddy must be taking a class."

On entering the house they kept Ullug's bag in guest house and proceeded towards the hall on the backside "Ullug! At present it will be a class for adults." In the meantime they heard voice of Mr. Khushroo.

"Your pain is the breaking of the shell that encloses your understanding. In order to remove, the dullness that has engulfed you, nature has given you one thing and that thing is your feelings of pain for others." Ullug stopped at the entrance. That sentence once again gave him memories of Farhana.

Pain! What is it? only one who suffers know that feeling.

Mr. Khushroo saw his son and Ullug coming to him. He looked at people sitting in the class room and said.

"Come on friends! my guest has come, now we will meet tomorrow at this time". When everyone left, keeping his hand on ullug's shoulder they came in living room.

"Come! My son come! How nice it would have been if you have brought your Abba with you? Many years have passed since we met each other".

"Uncle! Now he is also in advance age."

"How was your journey?"

"Journey! What shall I tell about this journey?. Life's journey has just now started. I am trying to reach to my destination. Let us see what happens now onwards?"

"Oh! You are talking like a philosopher. It is the influence of your Abba."

"Uncle! How do you know my Abba?."

"My son! I am also from Tashkent. At that time you were quite a small child. From there, I went to Kabul and as the war started we came here."

"Are you happy here?"

"My Son! motherland is always in my memory. But this country has given many more things. The biggest facility is to start Maderessa here and to teach Koran to children and adults. From where can they get someone to teach Koran to the generation that has been brought up in this culture?. My government over here has quite enduring behavior towards all religions, but recently gang wars are breaking out, so now, in name of religion Jehad is the movement due to which entire religion is blamed."

"Jehad is a sacred thing, and it is quite proper against injustice and non-Muslims".

"My son! First you have to decide what to call injustice. Is there an injustice from govt. to entire Muslim community.? Everyone is getting some facilities on principal of equality, one or two incidental cases cannot be termed as injustice."

"But uncle! English people by attacking on Muslim countries want to finish our entire community. Is it not injustice?".

"My Son! At present, Afghanistan and Iraq are on war path, it was because their govts. asked for protection, for their security. How can you call it injustice?."

Then even after these countries got independence why are they not moving out?" Still millions of people are getting killed by their bombings."

"My son! Afghanistan is in the control of Talibanis. There the rule is of terror rule. America has brought down Russian and its puppet govt., even then there is social and political disorder. But as long as Talibanis need Americans they will remain there. Same is the case with Iraq too."

"But not now. These countries have got support of Al-Qaeda and other Muslim countries."

"Then my son! Instead of fighting face to face or one to one fighting, fighting with terrorism of Al-Qaeda and killing innocent people do you think there will be any solution?"

"Oh uncle! Only the wearer knows where shoe pinches" Ullug's voice became harsh. Mr. Khushroo realized that ullug has got some pain. Some incident might have hurt him." At present he is talking with all seriousness, so Mr. Khushroo said smilingly. "My son! Al-Mustafa has said that when you are not taking pleasure of thoughts emerging from your conscious, at that time you, engage yourself in futile talks."

"Why are you saying so?"

"Because just a thought by itself is like a leisurely flying bird. When you put it in a cage, then his wings may open but cannot fly. Now leave this topic, you must have been tired. Go take bath and get fresh. At present you are going to stay here isn't it?"

"Please let us know purpose of your visit. Amir please take him to the guest room ".

At that time one young man saying "Salaam Alekum uncle" entered. Ullug turned back and saw him and he said with pleasure" Oh! Rushdi its you?."

"Do you know each other?" Asked Mr. Khushroo.

"Yes uncle! We met in Africa in connection with research work."

"Hum! Go, you also go in the room. You youngsters go and get busy. I have to go for prayers" When everyone left Khushroo started thinking. "We have to keep an eye on both of these young men. As per latest reports he met Al-Qaeda members in London often". Mr. Khushroo thought,

"I have to warn Fahad Mallik, father of Rushdi at St. Thomas Island."

"Oh! Ullug! I am really surprised seeing you here in London" said Rushdi while entering the room.

"Yes Rushdi! I have come here for some work." He thought it will not be proper to ask him in presence of Amir. He said "Amir! Thanks for all the help. Now I and Rushdi will talk about research. You might be getting late for your taxi business. If I need anything I will inform uncle."

Amir went and Ullug became serious and asked Rushdi, "What about your research work?".

"Just going on, Dr. Wellingdon is giving all assistance."

"Any new research?"

"No! Why?"

"What about samples of Chimpanzees you brought from Africa?"

"Yes! We brought samples with us. But you and Dr. Khoshev left early. Did you collect samples?."

Ullug was in a dilemma whether to commit but then said. "Rushdi I did collect samples along with Dr. Khoshev, but you know that Soviet Union is now divided. Dr. Khoshev died in Russia and what happened thereafter I do not know. I went back to Uzbekistan. Now I have joined one research center in Kabul. I want to proceed further in African research. So I remembered Dr. Wellingdon and came here thinking meeting him i will know something about it. Do you know anything?"

"Ullug! I am only a student. I will not know about secret research. In that matter Dr. Wellingdon has not said anything to me. I know about general matters only. My studies are over. In two-three months I will go back to St. Thomas to stay with my father. With the reference of Dr. Wellingdon. I have get a job in microbiology department of University. Research Center."

"Rushdi! Can I meet Dr. Wellingdon?"

"Yes! You can. I will take your appointment tomorrow only."

"Rushdi! Sometime I may need your help in that case can you help me from St. Thomas?"

"Ullug! That island is worth seeing at least once. When you come there you stay with me. I will talk to my daddy, he will be very happy."

After two days Ullug met Dr. Wellingdon in his Lab where he was received with warm welcome.

"Ullug Beg! Nice to see you again, what is going on? How come you are here?"

"Sir! Now I am head of Research Lab at Kabul University."

"Excellent! By the way what are the news of Dr. Khoshev?"

"Sir! You do not know that Dr. Khoshev died in one road accident?.."

"But in that case why these news were not made public world wide?. A famous scientist passes away like this and no news in any paper at all?"

"Sir! I left Moscow and on breaking away of Soviet Union all this happened."

"Then Ullug! What about the samples you collected from Africa?" Ullug got startled.

"Do not be surprised. It is the matter to be understood."

"Sir! I have no information about what happened to those samples. Now they are in control of Russian Govt."

"Ullug" said Dr. Wellingdon with all seriousness "What do you think Dr. Khoshev must have died in accident or the accident was intentionally."

"Why! You have any doubt?"

"Ullug! Those samples have been examined. As a result of that Dr. Khoshev met with his death."

"On what ground you feel like that?"

"Ullug! We also brought samples and its result gave us one deadly virus."

"Sir! What are you saying?" Ullug was quite excited.

"Yes Ullug! you are now a research scientist. On coming in contact with that virus, any person will die in three days. Those Chimpanzees died because of that only."

The blood contaminated by that virus is transferred by syringe or injection then one dies in three days., coming in contact with any fluid coming out of the body by perspiration or saliva, just by mere touch, close contacts also die.

"Sir! Then you have those virus samples?"

"All of them have been destroyed. How can you preserve such deadly virus? If it goes in wrong hands it will create massive destruction."

"Sir! Then what next?"

"We have sent these samples to America for further investigations, but I am worried about those viruses which have been left out in Russia."

"But Sir! What is the name of virus found by you?

If I know, then in my research if I find something similar, I can destroy them.

"Yes Ullug! You are right. Name of that virus is Ebola."

Ullug came out of that office, and a dangerous thought was taking shape in his mind. Ullug got one highly destructive weapon for revenge and he prepared a plan to go to Moscow. He came home with that deadly thought in his mind. Mr. Khushroo was addressing his class and saying "Please listen!"

"I will not like to sell pleasantness of my mind even for hundreds of thousands Dirham-money. Moreover tears of my inner conscious has rolled out from my sufferings, for those tears I will not like to take away someone's eternal joy."

Listening this, Farhana's innocent and beautiful face flashed in front of Ullug's eyes and anger in his heart got escalated. Pain to lose some one dear and near ones flashed like that of lava.

At that time Maulana Khushroo said further. "That's why friends I am telling you that as you believe that you achieved rewards by some wonderful activities done by you but that is not life. in such small pleasures. Life is only in two things. It is in pleasant smile coming out from loving mind, and, heart breaking painful tears. The balanced evaluation of a smile and tears is the purpose of life."

And he saw Ullug. Ullug's face was stern harsh but had tears in his eyes. Mullana thought, I must know the reasons for Ullug's pain. At that very moment Ullug left for his guest room.

CHAPTER 8

It was night time. Ullug was getting dispassionate.
There was no peace as Ullug's mind was totally disturbed.
Words of Maulana Khushroo were still echoing in his
ears. Maulana's words were testing his patience and
were instigating him to move away from his goal. He got
himself booked on Aero Float flight leaving after two days
for Moscow. But Maulana's words were disturbing his
mind, just like a force of cyclone in the ocean.

Maulana came to Ullug's room with a rosary in his
hand. Turning each bead, he came near Ullug's bed and
stood there. He got an intuition seeing Ullug sleeping
with closed eyes. There was an internal conflict between
the good and evil was going on in Ullug's mind. He was
getting ready to do something terrible. Maulana had a
divine personality. He can sense the vibrations of human
mind. Good or evil and thought how a religious minded
person like his friend Ismail Beg will be able to bear
misdeeds of his son?. He saw Ismail Beg's face on Ullug's
face.

As if echo of Maulana's thought was heard by Ullug,
he opened the eyes. Seeing Maulana standing near him,
he suddenly got up. Maulana set on a chair and said "My

son! Ullug! You are very restless. Can you tell me why? As if he was giving solace to Ullug, who felt as if his Abba was telling him something.He really felt good after so many days.

"No! Uncle! there is nothing of that sort" Normally a man stammers while telling a lie and he becomes restless.

"My Son! Are you planning to go to Moscow from here? Amir told me. Have you told him to keep his taxi ready day after tomorrow?"

"Uncle! At times I have to go there for research work from my center. Earlier I used to work there. I will go and meet my seniors ".

He looked down. While telling lies, one cannot meet an eye to eye. "Okay! My son! But now Soviet Union is divided. Communism is broken to pieces. At present, in Russia there is a hold of Mafia's and corrupt people. To steal technology of nuclear bomb and such killer weapons, every country is in a race. Be careful. Do you have any idea about how safe will be research lab over there?"

"No! Uncle! I am going to Moscow to ask for the help for my Research Center".

"You have to give bribe for that help isn't it? Who will give you money for that? Taliban Government or someone else . . . .?"

Ullug kept on looking at Maulana. This Maulana is not only a saintly person or God loving person but also knows world affairs. That is how he was keeping an alert eye on his son Amir. That is how Amir did not involve himself in any Muslim association.

"Yes! The help will be available from Government only."

"In return what your government is expecting from you?"

"In return? Uncle! To protect their people is their duty."

"In fact these Talibanis are the offshoot of America. Then how they become anti America?"

"Because American soldiers kill innocent people without any reason."

"And what Taliban government do? They obstruct progress. They are pushing the country backward. My Son! Prophet Mohammed gave rights to ladies even during Madina war. Then why Talibanis are creating obstructions against progress of women?. The world is taking a big leap making all round progress. Then why Talibanis are twisting and retarding Islam religion and teaching wrong concept of religion and make people to believe in religion with blind faith?."

"You are educated, you are intelligent. Be careful and do not be guided by their talks and be a weapon in their hands. My Son! Now myself and Ismail, how long we will live?. At this age, we cannot bear sufferings of our own loved ones. Please keep this thing in mind." Saying this he kept his rosary holding hand on Ullug's head. All good vibrations from rosary went down Ullug's body giving him a thrilling experience.

While leaving, Maulana gave one audio cassette to Ullug! "When your mind is disturbed at that time listen this Al-Mustafa's cassette. Very soon you will get sound sleep." Saying this he went away. Ullug kept on looking at the cassette. Slowly he placed that cassette in tape recorder and started,.

"When you hear a sound of love, give the reply without fail. Even if you find the path difficult, inaccessible, when love wants to engulf you, at that time submit yourself to love. Later on when thorns of life hurt you. Keep faith in language of love. Initialy that language may shatter your very dear dreams and spoil the same because path of love is full of heat as much as it is dignified and bright. As it awakens your imaginations, in same way it awakens the minutest atom of the body. Love is a purification process for everyone. All do not become punishable just you fail in love, or an untoward incident occur in your life."

And the cassette stopped. Ullug felt that the message in the cassette was for him. Love for Farhana was beautiful. In that love there is an element of sacrifice and forgiveness. And the raped body of Farhana came before his eyes and the lava of anger which was deeply buried in his mind came on surface. He became determined to fulfill his mission.

He got up in the morning. His face was serious. He made one telephone call "Osman! Are you still there isn't it? How is your research lab? Have you heard the news about Dr. Khoshev? What are you doing these days?"

"Ullug! After quite a long time nice to hear you. In two to three months after finishing my studies I will go back to my country Kazakistan. My job has been fixed! What are your news.?"

"I am coming to Moscow after two days. At present I am in London. Can I stay with you for some days!"

"Coming to Moscow? why not? Come! There is lot to Talk."

"Who is the head of research lab in place of Dr. Khoshev?"

"Mr. Muravaski."

"Oh"

"Why! Do you know him? One should be careful of him."

"Don't worry Osman" Saying this he gave his flight details."

Ullug kept recollecting Muravaski's face. He has still not forgotten his cruel face, which he saw during his train journey. He felt perhaps his mission may be fulfilled now.

There was an announcement in Russian Airlines Aero Float. "Flight landing at Moscow Airport. please fasten your seat belt." No difficulty was envisaged in immigration. For customs purpose there was only one suitcase and back pack. On coming out, he saw Osman standing at the gate to receive him. His face was brightened. Both of them set in a taxi. Ullug wanted to say something but Osman made him a sign not to talk. Ullug got surprised. Earlier when he was in Soviet Union, at that time nothing could be spoken due to fear of K.G.B. but even now that fear continues.

Taxi stopped near Osman's flat. Seeing the meter Osman gave money to the taxi driver. He tried to give money for the suitcase also. Taxi driver looked at Ullug with sharp eyes. Entering in the flat, Ullug asked "What is the matter Osman? Why you did not allow me to talk?

"Ullug! Presently here there is a lot of pressure from Mafia. Even the slightest doubt that you have come to Moscow for some work and you are a foreigner and from where are you coming, get all this information from taxi driver and you may be kidnaped. To get you released one has to pay a ransom they ask for. The hold of Mafia is right upto government level. There is no end to their wickedness. I wish my two months pass away without any trouble, I will be back home. Why have you come here?"

"Osman! I told you that Dr. Khoshev is no more. I want to meet Mr. Muravaski, please get his appointment."

"Ullug! He is highly influential. I have not seen anyone more corrupt person like him. He and security head Mr. Molotov have crossed all limits."

"No problem! He knows me. He will give me his appointment."

Ullug got appointment after two days. There was one day free and on that day he went with Osman to see his lab. Quite a few changes were noticed. Many new employees have joined. Every one was in uniform. Scene there was like a military barrack. Top floor was used by Muravaski for his office and offices of his administrative staff. Building was simple but when Ullug entered Muravaski's office seeing its interior decoration and luxury Ullug was astonished.

Muravaski kept on looking at Ullug who was standing in his office. Now there was no softness in him as a youth. He was looking a changed person.

"Yes!" Muravaski asked Ullug and he has not recognized him.

"Sir! I am Ullug! While traveling to Moscow from Tashkent we have met two three times. I was assistant to Dr. Khoshev".

Muravaski got stunned but very soon he got composed and wearing a mask of artificial smile he said "Oh! Ullug Beg? Come. We met after quite a long period. Where are you now?"

"I am at Research Center of Kabul University ".

"Nice! We need an efficient scientist like you."

"Yes! If Dr. Khoshev would have been then . . . .?"

"That means you do not know of Dr. Khoshev yet.?"

"Sir! Every one should get a generous boss like him. You may not be knowing, I went with him to Africa for research work."

This time a flash on Muravaski's face could not remain unseen. "Okay! You also went with him? Dr. Khoshev returned empty handed isn't it?"

Confused Ullug looked at Muravaski with piercing eyes.

"Sir! Has he not told you anything in connection with his research?"

"Research? No! I do not know anything."

"Who is the head scientist in your section? He might be knowing."

"I am everybody over here. You please take your seat here and tell me in detail about that research."

"We brought from there samples of Chimpanzee's saliva, blood, stool etc. for examining that why they suddenly die."

"You do not know anything about tests made by Dr. Khoshev."

Thinking for a while Ullug said.

"No! I left for Tashkent before that."

"Then what is the purpose of your coming here?" Muravaski was moving a pencil in his hand but his eyes were on Ullug's face.

Ullug got Muravaski's motive. He just smiled.

"By now you must have known the purpose of my coming here. I am head of the Research Center in Kabul, so I want to know."

"Right! So you want to know" that "thing" with a cunning smile on Muravaski's face he said."

"Sir! It has been said that enemy of the enemy is a friend."

"your enemy?"

"Not mine but ours, the Americans."

"Hum! Now you came to the point, what will you do after knowing that." And Ullug's face was all red with fury and anger and he said "With the test result of that virus I want to take revenge on Americans" Ullug said everything in detail.

"Good! Your aim is very high. I know very little about research but our scientists have made thousands of syringes by breeding that virus. They are kept in a safe place under lock and key. Name of that virus is new for me but by touching its blood, the person dies in three days. Do you know that?"

"Yes! This information is in England also. Though all virus have been destroyed there but I need them." Ullug said.

"What will you give in return?"

"As much money as you want."

"Do you have the capacity? From where you will bring millions."

"I will get" said Ullug.

"Wait! saying Muravaski clapped. One man came out from back side of his office."

"Colonel Molotov! This is Ullug Beg. He was working with Dr. Khoshev. He wants those virus." Their eye met and as if something was conveyed. Colonel Molotov set close to Ullug and kept his hand on Ullug. He extended his hand and took Ullug's hand in his hand, giving a pet he said "Young man! Everything has a price. Do you know that?"

Ullug extended his other hand towards the telephone. He looked to Muravaski and said "Can I make a call from here?. You can talk about money on other end." Colonel took away his hand. Ullug joined one number.

"I am Ullug Beg! A deal is to be done from Moscow. I want your concurrence." Saying this he gave phone to Muravaski.

"Hallo, who is there?" Hearing the name from other end, phone slipped of from Muravaski's hand. He managed to hold it back "Oh Sir! Osama Bin Laden in person."

"Yes! Without doing long talks spell out the amount. The same will be transferred to your account right now. On confirmation see that Ullug's work is done. If work remains incomplete then . . . .?"

"No! No! Sir! It can never happen like that. Colonel molotov is also here. He wants to say hello to you."

"Colonel! Do you remember the war?. You know how badly you were escaping away in the hilly terrain of karakoram and I gave you the shelter."

"Do you understand to return obligation? Not free! You will get money for that gesture. Hold on! The amount will be transferred in account of both of you instantly."

During this conversation Mr. Mulla Maqsood, an assistant of Osama gave orders to transfer funds to Moscow from bank of Riyadh the Capital city of Saudi Arabia.

On amount being transfered, Muravaski received phone call on second line.

"Sir! Your work is done."

Colonel Molotov and Muravaski heard that.

"Thank you very much Sir!" Saying this both phones were kept down.

Both of them were smiling. All got up, Colonel Molotov embraced Ullug. Muravaski said. "Ullug! Colonel! Tomorrow we have to go to the Safe Deposit Vault of Kremlin Security Bank. Ullug do you have time now?

"It is early afternoon. Shall we go now?"

"Yes! In this type of work there should not be any delay."

"Good! You have brought back-pack. We will definitely help you in killing your enemies."

Reaching Kremlin, everyone covered themselves with sterilized clothing, caps, hand gloves and with cloth cover on shoes. While opening the box, they found that syringes full of virus in frozen blood were kept at freezing temperature. Ullug kept all of them in his back pack, which was full of ice cubes to keep material safe.

All of them came out. They came back to Moscow. On reaching to Osman's flat Ullug said." Osman I want to leave from here at the earliest. Though I have a return ticket, but I do not want to take the risk of airport screening, so I will go by train. You drop me at Central Station."

"But Ullug! What is the urgency?"

"You will not understand. You only told me that here there is a danger from Mafia. I want to be away, and listen, suppose I might have to come again, in that case can I stay with you for few days?

"Do not worry for that. You tell me now where you want to go by train!"

"Osman! Please do not ask that please drop me fast."

While returning from Kremlin, Ullug had already made one plan.

CHAPTER 9

Ullug was looking at high-rise Central Railway Station of Moscow. This was one of the massive buildings which was built along with palaces and other mansions during Czar's rule and his monarchy. While entering in the station, he kept on watching activities and movements of innumerable people. Nobody was bothered about anybody. Everyone was walking rather running in their own tune. Czar's rule came to an end. There was a revolution, and Communism came to power. People got crushed under new rule. KGB's power was in full form but as it happens in every case, Soviet Union and Communism were broken down. People started running and dashing towards wealth and riches never seen before. Mafia and immoral corrupt people came into existence. Greed and avarice was seen on everyone's face. In Ullug's mind there was a flash of Maulana Khushroo and his words, "What have you got? What did you lose? To think and evaluate this, human being has no time."

Ullug entered in his coach. He got a window seat. With worried mind he set holding his back-pack to his chest, so no one can snatch it. Train signal was given, whistle blew up, brakes were released, and the way in which wheels got scratched with railway tracks, in the same way thoughts were crowding in Ullug's mind. What Abba must be doing at present? He made last call to him from Moscow. Abba was unwell at that time. But Ullug wanted to return to Kabul only after completing his mission. Will it be possible? Will he be successful? Will he be in a position to meet his father? He got dismayed by his own negative thoughts. Why is he getting negative thoughts, why he is not having peace of mind?. Will Allah not be with me in the task for which I am going?

He opened the window to feel comfortable. Soft breezes of flowing air brought pleasantness on his face, but cobweb of thoughts did not relieve him.

Caspian Sea!

He never dreamt that his journey will go towards Caspian Sea. Within himself, the Dark Sea of dejection was overflowing. In overflow of thoughts, there was a roaring sound of wild animals which only he could hear. He felt the heat of the air just like his ego. Some one breaks bodily or mentally with stress. Life is just wasted without purpose But he has a purpose to take revenge of Farhana's death, revenge of murder of fellow brothers. His destination is America. He wants to take revenge of assassination. But how far is the destination? He has feet but could not find pathway, when will he be coming out of this vicious circle? Will there be an end to his sufferings? Why a person of firm determination like him finds himself so helpless?

Abba will definitely be well soon. Thinking this, he saw outside the window. He took this long journey for not being spotted and caught by Mafia or corrupt officers. It was the journey of two nights to reach 'Azerbaijan' port on the Caspian Sea. Darkness of twilight was spreading.

Train purser came and gave blankets to all passengers. Cold air was blowing so he closed the window. But how to close window of one's mind? He was not in a position to bear heat of restlessness. Today he frequently remembered his Abba, and felt as if his Abba is like an old tree standing under hot sun, barren and with brittled branches. Now from where any bird will come there, sit on it and sing a song?. At present he is all alone helplessly waiting for death.

Will he be in a position to meet his Abba? In anxious moments, he thought that he was a love bird of his daddy. Will it be possible for him to go and sit with him? He felt as if a painful tide has engulfed him. In his mind there was a flash of Farhana's beautiful face. How innocent and bashful was she? She used to converse less, she was introvert, but she had an absolute faith in Almighty. Ullug and Farhana were not talking much even when they were together, but when she used to speak, it was like as if Al Mustafa a philosopher is speaking.

Sometimes Ullug used to ask. "Farhana! Why are you not talking?"

When she used to look at Ullug, he was experiencing a divine touch. Looking at him with her tender look, she used to say, 'Many times words crush love' Silence at times, opens words like flowers. To keep on seeing our reflections in each other's eyes with silence, there is an urge to talk but words are silently taken away by flowing air. Speechlessness creates one silent uproar in mind. In ears there is humming sound of birds. In our minds rosy fountains are going high, and both of us get wet in those fountains and voice of silence. Are they not our words? Are those acts of expression and experience not most charming?."

And while rewinding his own philosophy he spoke to himself! "Farhana! I will definitely take revenge and will pay you of that homage."

And he did not know when he went to deep sleep.

He got up in morning and saw that the Sandy Region has already started. The Western Bank of Caspian Sea was touching Eastern corner of Turky and North-East corner of Iraq. Being a desert like region, people were staying in Sandy Towns, away from all comforts of life. They were not even getting water supply. To get drinking water they had to dig pits in a dry river bed. That is the reason why Ullug selected this place. He reached to Azerbaijan port from where the desert land was entering Turkey. In those places few Turkish people and few Kurd people driven out by Sadaam Hussain were staying. Little away from Azerbaijan there was a village 'Arzurum'. Ullug selected that village. He hired one camel and started his journey towards "Arzurum".

The first thought came to his mind was that whether before reaching to Arzurum the experiment of the virus that he has brought with him can be conducted on camel driver? He wanted to stay there for three days. He hired one camel. Population in that village was also not much. It was like a big family of two / three thousand people. Arzurum had a railway station. Train was going straight to Ankara, the capital city of Turkey.

On first day of journey he reached to one Oasis. Under a palm tree camel was parked and camel driver said "Now in half a day we will reach Arzurum. Let camel take rest and we will have something to bite. You please sit here I will make arrangements for drinking water."

"Dear brother! Where will you go in search of water? I have brought one syrup bottle from Moscow, I also have something to eat, so let us also sit here."

As if life was approaching to an end of camel driver. How could he know that syrup brought by Ullug was blood of Chimpanzees containing virus was mixed in it!. After finishing his dinner and taking syrup, camel driver got up. Ullug took some water from his mineral water bottle and they started. It was half a day's journey, but before they reached 'Arzurum' camel driver vomited once.

They got down at road side guesthouse and camel driver was taken to the hospital where he was given medicine and was advised to take lot of glucose water.

On the next day there was a great festival in Arzurum of the Kurd and the Turkish people. Town being small one, the festival was for the whole village. Ullug got what he wanted. He took few blood samples and mixed them with incubated 'Moscow Virus'. He went to the festival with his back pack. On buffet-table, there were many varieties of food and drinks. Ladies, children and men wearing colorful traditional dresses were moving around, exchanging compliments to each other. As nobody was attentive, there was no need for Ullug to pierce the syringe and mix with food and drinks. Directly from the syringe he could mix some blood and virus with food and beverages. Festival was over with a happy note.

On next day of festival, children were the first casualty. Cough, vomiting and loose motion started. On third day camel driver was admitted in a hospital. Large number of adults were also admitted in that hospital. Officers thought that food poisoning was due to food items served during festival. No medical facilities were available is Arzrurum, so medical help was called from Azerbaijan.

Seeing health condition of people in Arzrurum Ullug was satisfied and he stealthily went to Railway station. He took a train to go to Ankara. Next day on reaching Ankara he folded his back pack and kept it in his suitcase in between other clothes to avoid problems of security check. If his suitcase gets cleared in luggage then there will not be any problem. His luggage got checked and cleared. He took a flight going to Antwerp.

At the time of scrutiny of luggage his name was not called so he had relief. But he was in suspense till his flight took off. He was relieved of anxiety when he reached Antwerp. He carried only one suit case. He removed his beard and mustache. Since he was looking like a tall, fair skin Britisher there was no inquiry in customs and on taking a taxi from airport he went to the residence of Aman Malik, brother of Rushdi's father Fahad Malik. From Rushdi Ullug had taken address of Aman Malik. Immediately when he started from Moscow he telephoned Rushdi and said "Rushdi I will have to go to Antwerp. One industrialist from Kabul is interested in diamond trade. Do you know anyone over there?"

"Oh! Since last many years my uncle has settled there. My father is also in diamond business. I will inform them about your Antwerp visit. They will help you in getting best quality diamonds".

"Then Rushdi will you please help me for one more thing? Can they send these diamonds directly to you at St. Thomas? Anyway since St. Thomas is under American rule, your father might have got some influence,

And Ullug reached Antwerp.

But in Arzrurum by the time third day was over, after eating that festival food, people started dying abruptly one after another. One medical team came from Azerbaijan, seeing so many people killed, they got shocked. As deaths were after the festival dinner, it was thought that food poisoning can be the only reason. Such news must be reported to the medical officers at Ankara. Medical director Dr. Pasha spoke "Such sad incidents are really painful, but immediately send samples of their vomit, stool etc to Ankara. We have to get samples examined."

By the time samples reached Ankara, one week was already over. But in developing country's research center where are the facilities of clinical examination of samples!. Director of Medicine telephoned to London.

He informed in detail to Dr. Wellingdon. He got startled. "Do one thing, send all samples to Home Land Security Research Center at Washington, and inform U.S. Ambassador about the emergency giving my reference. Perhaps my doubt may come true. But how is it possible? Was there any unknown guest? Please make discreet inquiries."

Zeba started to go to Research Center at Washington D.C. She was full of happiness and filled with tender emotions. Mysterious currents started flowing in Zeba's body. She started feeling sweet vibrations, What is this? Her heart started dancing, she was ready to give away something. Seeing Shekhar, her face looked more beautiful and became radient. She felt one kind of tenderness. She did not know that it is love and she is overwhelmed with it.

She entered the lab. Shekhar was deeply involved i in his work. She looked at him with naughty eyes and thoughts "Yes! This is called love." The moment Shekhar's assignment gets over she should go to India along with Shekhar or tell Sir Charles to arrange for Shekhar's Green Card and keep him here only.

But being stared by Zeba, Shekhar, got a feeling that someone is watching him and by seeing Zeba, tender expression came on his face. Keeping face down and taking both the hands behind his neck he stretched.

"This is called workout isn't it?".

"What are you looking at?" Shekhar asked.

"Your body! It reveals loveliness of your athletic body."

"In recent times you have started using colorful and ornamental words."

"What to do? One young lady wants to hear such things from a youth. But you are mean!"

All of a sudden Shekhar became serious and said. "Zeba I understand and I am also having similar feelings for you. But what will be the end?"

"Why? What can be the end of love? Let both of us unite."

"Zeba! I am son of a conservative Brahmin family from South India, how my parents will agree?

"Do your parents understand in love?"

"Zeba! You should understand their psyche of mind."

"OK! I believe what you say. But what do you wish?"

"Zeba! You know my feelings"

"Then everything else does not matter, I will take care of your parents. Now what have you to say!"

At that time lab Director came there. "Miss Khalid! It is good that you are here! Are there any news from your department?

"Yes Sir! The incidence that has happened in desert area of Turkey has startled everyone, as, massive deaths have taken place there and for that Turkish Govt. is worried."

"And Zeba! Task of examining those samples has been given to Mr. Reddy."

"Okay! That is the reason why he is so busy! But Sir . . . ."

"You want to say that he is not devoting sufficient time to you, isn't it?" The director was aware of love relationship between Shekhar & Zeba.

I feel happy today by seeing working skill of both of you. Tell me what can I do for you?"

Zeba got a golden opportunity. "Sir!" She said in an artificial sad voice, and her words brought desired affect.

"Sir! In two months time Mr. Reddy will have to go back to India."

"Why? Still his presence is very much required here ".

"His working Visa is getting over."

"Then we will get it extended ".

"Instead of that Sir!" Zeba blushed and said "Sir he should get Green Card."

"Excuse me" Saying he lifted the phone.

"Oh! Mr. Christie? Yes! Mr. Reddy is working on that only. The moment I get report, I will let you know. But yes! I am informing you that Mr. Reddy's Working Visa gets over in two months. What should we do?"

"No, No! Instead of extending his Visa can Green Card be arranged?. He is with us since last five years,"

And looking to Zeba he said with smile that, "Even agent Zeba also wants that way."

"Tell her that it will be done that way only. Please ensure that he makes application today." Director put down phone and said, "Congratulations Miss. Khalid! Green Card will be arranged for Mr. Reddy. He has to send his application today only."

"Thank you very much Sir!" Zeba coyly said.

"Yes! Mr. Reddy! the tissues and samples received from Turkey are examined?" Inquired the director.

"Sir! Zeba said "Why do you want to inspect? From the report only food poisoning is confirmed."

"Yes! But officers from Ankara had a talk with Dr. Wellingdon at London who has a doubt that as per his earlier report en-mass killings may be due to . . . ."

"Ebola."

Cutting his sentence Shekhar said "Sir!. Diagnosis is same Virus—Ebola is the cause for their deaths".

Director and Zeba both got shocked and Zeba said. "Sir how virus could have reached there?

"It may be work of some unknown person or a guest. Dr. Wellingdon gave shocking news that samples that he brought from London, similar samples Dr. Khoshev took to Russia."

"Took away, you mean stole them?"

"Yes! Dr. Khoshev was killed in an accident and at that time his assistant Mr. Ullug Beg was with him".

He is at present head of research lab at Kabul. Mr. Christie while inquiring with our Ambassador at Kabul came to know that Mr. Beg is traveling at present.

"Zeba! You are FBI agent, Mr. Christie will give you some assignment in this matter. Be on guard."

On the same day Ullug came to Antwerp to move ahead, his second phase of his mission and to take his journey further he telephoned Rushdi at London.

"Rushdi, I have reached Antwerp, when are you going to St. Thomas?"

"I am leaving tomorrow for St. Thomas"

"OK! Then after reaching there you talk to your uncle about my diamond business, so my task will be easy. I will talk to you once you get my parcels."

"Yes! Ullug! But there is one sad news."

CHAPTER 10

Rushdi what's news?

"Ullug! You are out of Kabul for quite some time. Moreover, you have gone by train from Moscow somewhere near Caspian Sea, so in Antwerp you will not know what happens in Afghanistan.

On knowing details Ullug got startled. For a moment Ullug was shocked but knowing details he was fuming in anger to take revenge. He got one more reason to retaliate and take revenge.

American Ambassador residing in Kabul was in dilemma and shocked on receiving a phone call from his military chief. He immediately rang up Washington D.C. "President Sir! You must have received a phone from military chief, please tell us what is to be done now? Orders have been issued."

Putting the phone down Ambassador kept on thinking that in last few months Talibanis' aggression has crossed all limits.

Proclamation was issued "Everyone has to follow Sheri at—Law. Ladies have not to go out for work or service. When they come out from their homes they must be fully covered with burkhas—veils. Girls have not to go school for study and, separate schools have been built for boys and girls. Everyone has to go to learn Koran. If any married woman is found keeping extra marital relations, then she will be punished to death, and that too in what manner . . . .?"

"Hamid! Today your wife had gone to the market to buy vegetables. While buying vegetables she saw one American soldier staring at her.

"But she must have put on burkha, then how do you know that s he was staring?"

"That soldier made some sign, and your wife went behind the tent and the soldier gave her some money. She bought vegetables from that money."

"But Amjad! my household affairs are not run by my income only, so she was sad and so the soldier showing mercy might have given some money"

"Are you taking side of your wife? That vegetable vendor must have informed Mulla Omar. Please be on guard."

Hamid when he came home knew the truth. His wife said her children did not get any thing to eat for last four days. She went to buy vegetables, but the prices were four times higher than the normal price. She was helpless. She started sobbing and crying loudly. That soldier showed mercy on her and gave some money to her to buy vegetables and grocery, only after that, children enjoyed their lunch.

In the meantime, four Talibanis came with rifles and without telling anything, they picked her up at gun point. Pushing her children away they took her to a central place in Kabul.

People were forced to watch the scene. Head of the group of four Talibanis started giving lecture. "Brothers!

Today you will see the justice done by Talibanis. This woman is unholy. She is keeping relations with American soldier betraying her husband., what should be done with such woman? Can God the Almighty forgive her! If you will not punish her, God will be angry with you."

"Yes, Yes! She deserves punishment" illiterate people are prepared to do anything in name of God, and all the people who assembled there formed a circle. Neither Hamid got a chance to say anything nor his wife's humble requests were heard. "I am innocent, I am innocent". Big big stones were moving from one hand to the other and one Talibani hit stone on that woman's head. She got unconscious. In her unconscious state she was beaten with whip. Subsequently one person after another threw stones at her. Lady died on the spot. Children got terribly shocked. After every one left that place, Hamid took dead body of his wife and came home.

Moreover, in war against Russia, Talibanis lost heavily. Quite a few children became orphans. One orphanage was opened on outskirts of Kabul and one Afghan was looking after it. Talibanis and Mulla Omar came to know about that place. There were about three hundred orphans out of which most of them were boys. Women and girls were prohibited to come out of their homes.

Every fifteen days Mulla Omar's man used to come there for giving some money, and he used to pick up one boy from the orphanage. After finishing govt. job, religious heads were meeting together for marry making. At that time jingling anklets were wrapped on the boy's legs and he was made to dance. After the dance he was handed over to govt. officers for immoral purposes. After some time the boy used to die or he was sent back to the orphanage.

Slowly, Talibanis started harassing American soldiers. As American soldiers were being harassed, orders came from Washington and the mission of attacking Talibanis got initiated. Before that, help from some leaders of people' group was solicited and war started. Against America's ultra modern arms and ammunitions, Talibans were no match. In name of Islam, Al-Qaeda chief Osama Bin Laden did receive arms and ammunitions from Islamic countries, but before these ammunitions reached at the required place, it was not possible to stop or obstruct American attack.

After meeting Farhana's father, Ismail Beg was returning to his home. At that time he was surrounded at Kabul Circle between Talibanis and American soldiers. Due to mustache, beard and traditional turban, American soldiers could not separate him from other Talibanis. In incessant bullet firing, Ismail Beg was killed along with other innocent Afghans, Talibanis could not encounter sudden violent attack.

During that time one wing of American army made violent attack on Omar Mulla's palace and Talibanis started fleeing. Some of them ran towards Khyber ghat but most of them went to Swat Velley on Pakistan border.

With American help temporary caretaker govt. was formed. Hearing his father's death, shocked Ullug was speechless. but was fuming with anger. Now he determined to put his plan in action to go to St. Thomas Island.

One man with a piece of cloth covering his face, a turban on the head and wearing a long loose traditional dress, and who also was tall and stout entered in Mallik and Mallik's jewellery store.

Rushdi had returned since a week. He was behind the counters and was checking diamond packets. Magnifying glasses were lying on the table. On counters opposite to each other two Muslim and two American ladies were taking care of customers.

That man gave a contemptuous look towards women and Rushdi came forward. One lady who was free came to the counter and asked "May I help you?"

"You do not know Urdu? Salam Alekum" said Mulla Maqsood.

"Walekum Salam! Any assistance?"

"No."

Listening this conversation, Rushdi stopped checking diamonds and raising his eyes looked at that man. He got startled looking to his funny dress. As he has seen photographs in the posters of Al-Qaeda terrorist organization's accomplice he could know that the man is from Al-Qaeda clan.

"Salam Alekum! Dear brother" saying this he greeted Mulla.

Mulla was pleased to see politeness of young man of 25-30 years of age.

"Young man what is your name?'

"Rushdi".

"Your daddy—Abba . . . . ?"

"He is in his office" saying this Rushdi started walking towards his father's office.

"Rushdi, I want to talk to him in person. Can I go inside his office? I have some private matter to discuss. My name is Mulla Maqsood".

Rushdi told this to his father Fahad Mallik. Hearing his name, Fahad got startled. Mulla Maqsood? Right hand of Osama Bin Laden? The most wanted person? The man whom American Govt. is desperately searching. How could he come upto St. Thomas Island?

As per latest information Al-Qaeda has spread its network in Pakistan, Yemen, Sudan, Somalia. Having big political instability in Sudan and Somalia, Yemen and Pakistan became Al-Qaeda head quarters. As per last report Mulla Maqsood was in Yemen. Why has he come here? In St. Thomas Island, Muslim population was in large number. Some of them were very rich and financially sound. Fahad Mallik was aware of the movement of Terrorists and so he had hated them.

"Rushdi! Send him inside and close the door, but keep on listening our conversation. Call our security guard and get him checked. He might have come with ammunitions or grenades with him so tell him that there is a law in this country that security check is a must for any visitor."

"Fine, Abba!"

"Maqsood Sir!" As per law of this country you can go inside only after security check. Will you mind that?"

"No, No! While coming in, security check is done of all visitors. I was also checked, even then you can get it done once again."

Maqsood was a cunning person. He had studied laws of almost all the countries and was well versed in them. Unless it was needed by Al-Qaeda or Taliban he was not making use of arms.

After security check, Maqsood entered office of Fahad Mallik. He had collected full information about Mallik. Years back he came to St. Thomas Island from Pakistan. He developed his jewelery business quite well. His relatives were settled in London and Antwerp. Diamonds from whole world used to come to Antwerp, examined and were dispatched to other countries from there. Fahad Mallik was a religious minded person. Since last many years he was staying in America. He was an honest citizen of America. He was against terrorist activities of recent times. St. Thomas was a small island. It was a beautiful place without civil disorder or terrorism. Hindus and Muslims were staying as families. All festivals were celebrated together. Fahad Mallik by and large understood the purpose of Maqsood's visit. Fahad Mallik was a truthful person having strong and determined mind.

Mulla Maqsood entered the office of Fahad Mallik who got up to greet him. Seeing his outlaw type appearance, Fahad Mallik started thinking. How could this man passed through the security check at the airport? But terrorist have many avenues.

"Salam Alekum, Maqsood Sir! Please come" His language was full of sweetness. Maqsood looked at Fahad's piercing eyes. Fahad was well built and should be about fifty five years in age. He was well built and healthy".

"Oh! Fahad Sir! Walekum Salam" saying this he took a seat "You are very well settled here and you are also leader of Muslim community here."

"Allah malik-master" Fahad said raising his hand to sky.

"Let his grace reach to us also" said Mr. Maqsood.

"I am a common man and I am insignificant."

"If you wish you can do a lot."

"Yes! I am ready if it is a business related talk."

"You do not think of religion. only business?"

"Religion is gift of Allah. In this country when we assemble in a Mosque we talk about Koran. Moreover we have to be in tune with local culture also."

"On counters outside I saw that girls are working in this store. You do not feel that our religion is telling that women should stay at home only and look after their husband and children."

For a while Fahad kept on looking at Maqsood and then said "I think meaning of Sheri—at Law has been twisted. Prophet has said that a woman, besides being a wife and the mother, she also has to fulfill worldly duties along with her husband. If need be they should also be capable to make use of arms for self defense. God has given them heart and the mind. Then can a man stop their thinking process?"

"I feel that you have not followed religion properly. The place for women is in home only."

"Good! Every one has his own opinion what one should do depends on his own choice."

"No! Things must be done as per religion's verdict."

"The meaning of religion is derived by men and women as per their thinking. Now tell me, what can I do for you?'

"Do you believe in Jehad?"

"Yes! Jehad is a sacred activity. To raise voice against injustice and oppression, is called Jehad."

"You said the truth. We have raised our voice against injustice and oppression. We want your help."

"You used the word 'We'! We means?"

"We means entire Islamic world"

"What injustice and oppression has been done to Islamic world?"

"Why don't you understand?. The great power America is enjoying absolute power and uses the same as per its sweet will."

"Oppression has been in which country and on which community?.."

"Iran, Iraq, Afghanistan and many more."

"Are these countries not capable of defending themselves? Are you chief of these countries, so long as their defense is concerned?

"Do you know who am I?"

"Yes! Little while ago you said that you are Mulla Maqsood. Do you know the meaning of Mulla?" He is God's assistant and humble disciple. God always asks to forgive, what do you say?"

"I am right hand of Osma Bin Laden. You have to help us for Jehad."

"What tyranny and oppression have been done on Osama Bin Laden".

"He has raised Jehad for Islam."

"To which place he belongs to? Saudi Arabia? Why Saudi Arabia is not helping him? Is he a citizen of that country?"

"Yes! But Osama has raised Jehad for entire Islamic world."

"Has the Islamic world lodged any complaint? Justice is demanded by one person who has suffered from injustice, then you cannot say that injustice has been done to the whole world. In this world every one has to find out solutions of their problems. The word like Jehad should not be put in a shameful position by killing innocent people in name of Jehad. Even then I feel that those people who raise Jehad and do Jehad in real sense, for them there will always be my support. You do one thing, come to mosque in the evening and meet community people, take their opinion and thereafter tomorrow we will meet in my office for further deliberations. My son Rushdi has arranged one sightseeing program for you Mr. Maqsood.

Rushdi came in and said "Maqsood Sir! Please come, I will give you details about places where you should go for sightseeing".

Maqsood got up. He stared at Fahad without giving a blink. He felt as if he is standing in front of a hard rock. While coming out he looked at the innocent face of Rushdi and thought that many innocent people have been mislead, can this boy also not be mislead?"

"Maqsood Sir! Car is ready for you. In evening car will pick you up for going to mosque."

Maqsood understood that Rushdi has listened full conversation with Fahad. Hope was raised in his mind that he can deceive Rushdi. In evening car came to take him to the mosque. He was looking to grand building of mosque. The community residing here has built this beautiful mosque from their earnings. Maqsood washed his hands and feet before entering in the mosque. He bowed his head in respect and heard the voice of Fahad.

"Now let us leave talking about the grandeur of Allah the Almighty. Instead of searching Him, let us talk of Him who is staying within us. Quite often we are talking of Divine music but have you ever thought of Nightingale singing in our courtyard?".

It means we should think of and take care of people around us. Allah is there to take care of the world, leave it to Him. There is no need for every one to take care fot that. If everyone of us tries to understand each other, understand the neighbor, then it will look like one God is embracing another God. Instead of misguiding innocent people by fright and by fear, in name of religion using power, money and greed for self interest, people should be made to understand true meaning of religion. In all of us there is fragrance, sweet smell, and the astute power which are the seeds of humanity. We ourselves are freely moving birds, flowers, sweet smell of mother earth, sea currents and sweet sound. There is nothing in this world except our existence.

Mulla Maqsood kept on listening thinking of this simple holy man. As long as he is there, Will there be any possibility to expect funds from this man or community for Jehad? He took a seat in the car. Seeing Rushdi driving the car he said "Rushdi you heard the conversation between me and your Abba. What do you think about it?"

"Maqsood Sir! Abba stays here since last so many years. He is faithful to this country. But young generation wants to fly out of this stagnant place. I am President of Youth forum here. All young men are educated but we don't get a good path finder."

"Rushdi tomorrow I will come to your store once again and I will have a final conservation with your Abba. If your young friends find time then bring them to the hotel. We will share some religious thoughts.

Next day Mulla Maqsood came to Fahad Mallik's store with very little hope, but he had high hopes in Rushdi. He talked to some young people who.

started thinking about these new ideas,

Fahad Mallik came to know that Rushdi took some young people to meet Maqsood. But there were few talks only, he welcomed Maqsood.

"Fahad Sir! Your yesterday's lectures were eye opening for me. Our organization desperately needs learned people like you. Please help us."

"Look! Mr. Maqsood I am an American Citizen and have taken an oath to be faithful. How can I cheat and betray them. Your organization is a threat to America. I cannot do anything against the law of this country".

In the meantime Rushdi came there and said. "Abba! I have talked to you about my friend isn't it? He is interested in diamonds. He has met uncle in Antwerp. He has purchased diamonds, and with his and our order that we have given, are to be sent by parcel which will take few days. During that period he wants to stay with us for few days and for that he wants your permission. He is my close friend".

Fahad took phone and said. "Yes! My son he is your friend and we never deny even a stranger as a guest. Has he said from which country he is? Uzbekistan? Is he working in Kabul? In research center then how he got interested in diamonds? Okay, diamonds are required for a Kabul industrialist?"

Maqsood got alert hearing about kabul.

"Yes my son! Come with pleasure. My doors are open for a guest. You are welcome! One minute! What is your name? Ullug Beg.? Please come." Fahad mallik put down the phone he did it to Antwerp.

Listening Ullug's name Maqsood felt happy. He got up and while coming out he said "Rushdi! I want to meet your friend."

CHAPTER 11

Suleman Mallik kept on looking at Ullug, a tall stout, and handsome young man in traditional dress. His face was harsh but eyes were very soft.

Suleman looked outside from glass window of this office in his Jewelery store in Antwerp. After proper security check only anyone was allowed to enter in the store and again there was a security check at the time of his exit.

Ullug was fully checked when he entered the store. He came in and seeing the grandeur of this ultra modern store, he could realize what is called pomp and shaw-luxury. Rushdi's uncle was there but he did not know Ullug. He went to one counter. One young English Lady came near him and asked "may I help you?"

"Yes! I want to buy best quality diamonds."

"Any particular brand name like D. Bears Company of South Africa or of once upon a time Tanzania based Williamson Diamond Mines or those of Cartier's." Are you interested in diamonds only or other precious gems such as Amethyst, Garnet or famous Tanzanite.

"Please give me samples of all of them" said Ullug. During that time, intercom connection in the Suleman's office started functioning Mr. Mallik while sitting in his office used to hear conversation of the clients coming there. Ullug separated certain diamonds, Tanzanite and Amethyst. He took one diamond in his hand and raised the same to see it in light coming from outside.

"Mam! How much is inclusion in this? How many grades will be there? S.S. one or two? In light if many colors are formed in a diamond you can tell the intensity of defect is formed then how defective is that diamond? Why this Tanzanite given by you is dark blue one? You don't have one of light, blue color? Or with the variation in carets, the color of diamond changes?

Suleman Mallik got the point that Ullug was well informed and has good knowledge about diamonds. On intercom Suleman told "Please send him in my office."

Ullug entered in Mallik's office and set in front of him.

"Where are you coming from?.."

I am from Kabul, originally from Uzbekistan."

"Kabul! What are you doing there?"

"I am head of University Research Center."

"Research? My nephew is also very much interested in research. His name is Rushdi."

"Is he the same person who was with Dr. Wellington in London?"

"Yes! Do you know him?.."

"Yes! We went together to Africa."

"Oh! After completing his studies he has gone back to his home at St. Thomas Islands".

"Oh! St. Thomas? I am also going to St. Thomas at his place ".

"Oh! It is very very good. He is my brother's son. He also has jewelery store. I supply them diamonds from here."

And there was a telephone buzz.

"Walekum Salam! My son! You are going to leave hundred years. Just now I was talking with your friend Ullug Beg! He is going to come to you at St. Thomas."

"He has come to buy diamonds for some industrialist in Kabul. Please inform my brother that his order is ready and I will send the parcel in a day or two to him."

"Uncle! Please take care of Ullug. He does not know anyone over there. He has to come here with diamonds which is risky. With the parcel of our order can his parcel also be sent at our address?"

"Of course! Rushdi, i can do that much for you isn't it?" Saying this he put down the phone.

"Have you heard what Rushdi is saying? Your parcel will also be sent by us."

"Can I call you uncle? I have other diamonds also, hence I will take my today's purchases to my hotel room and after keeping all together I will make one parcel and bring it here tomorrow."

"Ullug! You called me uncle isn't it? Then how can you stay in a hotel now that too with this risk? We go to the hotel from here, collect your luggage and come to my place. You have to stay with me."

Ullug kept on looking at this soft hearted person. How quietly he has put trust in me. Are the militants not taking advantage of such people? In the meantime Suleman said "Ullug! Have you heard the news about Kabul? Americans have driven out Talibanis. One dangerous rule has come to an end. What are your plans to go back to Kabul?."

Tears came in Ullug's eyes. He said "Uncle what will I do there? I have lost my would be wife and I have lost my Abba. They were killed by Americans. I don't know when I will go back to Kabul"

how truly but unknowingly one utters his own destiny! ."

"Excuse me my son. I have hurt your feelings. You can stay here peacefully as long as you wish. At St. Thomas Fahad will keep you like his son. First compose yourself and then decide,. Ok?"

Ullug collected his diamond packet and went to hotel along with Suleman Mallik in his car and taking his luggage from the hotel he came to Suleman Mallik's posh-luxurious residence. After finishing evening meals he went to his room. From suitcase he took out his back-pack and kept on looking at his deadly luggage. He visualized the face of his diseased father. Memory of dead ones is more painful then actual death. Death's blow can only be cured by time and God the Almighty. But in Ullug has lost two loved ones and those wounds were still fresh. Will those wounds be healed by passage of time?. Once Farhana had sung in front of Ullug one poem of Sufi Poet Rumi.

In moonlight I see the wounds given by you. The flowers given by you have withered out, but I keep them fresh with my tears. The unsung songs flow in one non-stop music. One such composition by an immortal singer Noorjehan is as under :

> "Moonlit night, Moonlit night
> When whole world is sleeping
> I am awake and talk with stars
> Oh moonlit night." HE translated it in his
> own language.

(chandani raten, chandani raten, sab jag soye, mai jagu, tarose karu baten).

Pushing away the tears and remembering his loved ones, Ullug took out deadly luggage, namely syringes and incubation dishes, and arranged them with diamond packets. Virus were dried but he knew how to revive and convert the dried virus into life. He kept ready the parcel which he was to send next day morning through Suleman uncle. Now therefore nothing was to be afraid of airport security check. Feeling light hearted he slept peacefully to start for his next journey.

How was his next journey?

How ignorant js human being of the future?

For a while his stormy mind got cooled down and he slept peacefully. But that peace was just momentary. He started getting restless. Not being able to bear the heat, he got up from his bed. He was uneasy. Was it some kind of a premonition? Why after so many days memories of Abba and Farhana are tormenting him!. Abba used to say "My son please be careful of the people with whom you are working. Don't be misled". After Farhana's death he told Ullug not to trust Talibanis. But now he got himself so involved with Al-Qaeda, that he was ready for real Jehad.

But the meaning given by Maulana Khushroo of word Jehad was making Ullug quite uncomfortable. If Prophet has given importance to forgiveness then what is the purpose of Jehad?

Why the same word is used as an alternative to terrorism?. Is it because nobody understands the real meaning of word Jehad? So the use of Sacred word like Jehad is interpreted for disgraceful activity and for self interest? For the first time Ullug got confused.

For the first time he sat in his bed in a prayer—Namaz like position with both the legs bent and keeping both the hands right upto his face Ullug started talking with himself.

"Oh God please call back this entirely spread fire. This quiet cool, and sharp fire-hatred is killing me by deep despair. Please give me the strength to be successful in my mission."

As if his prayer is heard, his mind started getting calm. He lied down on the bed and fell asleep.

In the morning Suleman sitting on breakfast table told "Ullug! My son! How will you handle diamond packets while going to Kabul from St. Thomas? How will you take them?"

"Uncle! I will parcel them to the persons for whom I have purchased diamonds. I have got some work with Rushdi in his research center. So I have to stay at St. Thomas."

"No problem. Fahad is a very kind hearted person. Keep faith in Allah. You have done your duties without any self interest. You will be successful. But be careful, Today both the parcels will be dispatched from here. We have established our business here for last many years. We have got lot of acquaintance and influence. All members of Royal family buy their diamonds from us only. That much reputation we have earned."

"Uncle please don't worry. Thanks for getting my work done. If my Abba would have been alive, then he would have been quite happy and would have felt relieved by knowing you and Fahad uncle." Saying this Ullug got emotional.

"Ullug! My son! By knowing you I understand that you have got a clean heart, but some times I see your eyes fuming with anger, Any special reason?"

Ullug narrated the whole incident of Farhana.

My son! I understand that anybody can get angry in such a situation. But all people do not become enemies by one instance. Be careful that no one should take your anger as your weakness and may misuse the same.

Ullug kept on looking at Suleman. Is it so that the noble people can read cruel people's mind?.

"Ullug! Please don't worry, one has to fulfill mission of his life."

"Please listen! I have got one beautiful book. May I give it to you? You will have good time pass during your journey."

"Salam Alekum"! Hearing this from the adjoing seat Ullug got startled. As one has to reply Ullug said Walekum Salam".

"Where are you going?"

"St. Thomas, and you?"

"I am going to Miami"

"Which place do you belong to originally?"

"Originally from Uzbekistan then to india but I came to America as a refugee. What about you?"

"Originally from Uzbekistan, Tashkent."

"Then we are from the same place. From St. Thomas please come to Miami. My name is Ajmal Kureshi."

"Since how long are you there?"

"About fifteen years."

"Are you in business?.."

"I have a grocery store and sale of meat is on higher side because as Muslim community is in substantially large number. What about you?"

"I am a professor in a research center at Kabul".

"Kabul? There is a revolution over there. I stay in America. I am an American citizen. But the way in which America is heading towards enmity becomes unbearable, But how is it possible for us to keep enmity with a crocodile-America when you to have to stray in the same water?"

"You are right. I have never come to America. St. Thomas Island is under American rule, hence, I have got Visitor's Visa. Can I come to Miami?"

Ullug started thinking about executing a new plan.

"You can definitely come. Please come and be our guest. My wife Amina will be happy. More so because you are from Uzbekistan."

And Ajmal Kureshi closed his eyes for rest.

Ullug took out the book.

"One who does not face challenging situations he can never win. You do not enjoy what you have, but become more greedy for something more to get.

Ullug smiled. It is true that he is also running for such greed and in that run he met Ajmal Kureshi and he felt that his mission will be successful. His plan started shaping well. It must be God's wish that he should be successful and that is why he met Ajmal. Closing the book he became more determined. He kept the book in his handbag. Some courtesy talks were done and Ullug asked.

"Ajmal Sir! Recently militants are harassing America. Has America not made a mistake by starting war in Afghanistan?.."

"They have done a mistake but what can they do.? Talibanis are their own creation. How long can they suffer?"

"But they are killing innocent Muslims. Are you not unhappy about that?"

"It is painful but by sitting here what can we do?"

"Have you heard about Al-Qaeda?"

"Yes son! I have heard about it. But we are small people and we live happily and peacefully then what else we have to do?"

"If someone comes to you and asks help for Jehad will you give?".

"Sure"

"If I ask?"

"I will definitely do. What is to be done?"

"Nothing much. I want to send one parcel to Miami from St. Thomas. But since I don't know anybody over there I was worried, so I asked you."

"What are the contents in that parcel?".

"I have purchased diamonds from Antwerp to be taken to Kabul. Unless there is someone who is trustworthy, nothing can be done."

"This is my card and my address. You can definitely send the parcel to me and be our guest. You ring me before arrival so I can pick you up at the airport."

"Ajmal Sir! Thank you so much."

"I will ring you from St. Thomas after one week".

Plane landed at St. Thomas Airport. While leaving the aircraft Ullug said "Good bye—khuda hafeez" to Ajmal Kureshi.

He was not aware that he has to use same words once again.

CHAPTER 12

Ullug has never seen such a beautiful place ever before.

Airport of St. Thomas Island's capital city Charlotte Emily was also equally modern. With this airport, Ullug was comparing airports of Pakistan which have become camps of militants from Afghanistan and Uzbekistan.

Ullug went inside the Airport. His baggage came quite safely on baggage claim carousel. He went to the lounge. As Rushdi has not reached there, Ullug set on a sofa chair and picked up a book lying on side table and started reading. That book was on travel and tourism.

In the year 1493, Columbus discovered this island. It was known as Caribbean Island as it was in the Caribbean Sea. Prior to year 1500 B.C. inhabitants of that island were Sibonis, after Sibonis Aravacs came and came caribz.

There was a beautiful sea shore on the island's capital city. The Dutch people established one company known as Dutch West India Co. and slowly conquered the whole island but this island was modernized by Americans, when they took it in the year 1917. Island was surrounded by sea. But the land was uneven and houses were built on the slopes of small hills. Natural green meadows were there all the time. Due to Tropical temperature the island was remaining green and fresh. It's modernization started after America took it over. Population on this island was about fifty thousand people. There were many sugar plantations and to work on such plantations their owners bought slaves. Along with Africans, the laborers came from India in which there were Muslims also.

"Ullug" an anxious voice was heard "I m sorry. I am late as there were many customers in the store."

"No problem! By the time you arrived here, I collected some information about your island." Both of them came out and Ullug kept on seeing the prosperous island, and said "Rushdi! Your city and island both are beautiful."

"Ullug! Daddy is staying here since last twenty five years. He came here as a laborer to work in sugar plantations from Hyderabad city in India. Gradually he joined this Jewelery store. God the Almighty was very kind to him. He was very much interested and knew diamond business. Owner of jewelery store was a Dutch business man. Seeing daddy's keen interest he was very happy. That Dutch man, Mr. vanderberg was staying alone. Even after Dutch Govt. went away from here he continued to stay here. From his death bed Mr. vanderberg took a promise from my daddy that he will look after the store. As of even now daddy is sending one third of his profits to the family members of Mr. vanderberg."

In the meantime they came to a slope of a hill. An Asphalt road was built till the top of the hill. Car was slowly going up the hill. "Rushdi! Why you took the car on the hill?" Asked Ullug.

"Ullug! Affluent people of this island construct houses and cabins and stay here. My daddy has also built one bunglow here. We will go there prior to other places."

They were having pleasant feelings as they were going up the heights seeing fabulous flow of the sea on all sides on the way. On reaching at the top of the hill, entering the house Ullug got astonished seeing posh drawing room in Fahad's bunglow.

Noorjahan's—the famous singer's melodious voice was relaying soft tunes in the room.

> "O Moonlit night, Moonlit night
> When whole world is sleeping,
> I am awake and talk with stars
> O moonlit night ".

"Ullug! Daddy is enchanted by Noorjahan's voice, you also must have heard her name."

"Yes Rushdi! In Kabul, Afghanistan and in Pakistan there is a big craze for Indian films and singers."

Rushdi took Ullug to the guest room. Seeing the packet lying on the table, Rushdi said "Ullug! Uncle has sent your parcel from Antwerp." There was a deadly flash in Ullug's eyes.

"Very good!" Saying this he caressed the parcel and felt as if he has touched a soft skin of a snake.?

"And yes! Someone was inquiring about you and said that he wants to meet you."

"Here on this island?" Ullug said with an astonishing face.

"Some one by name Mulla Maqsood wants to meet you."

He has liked this hilly place very much. I have taken him to see caves around here."

Ullug got the point, why the caves., and, visualized as if Bin Laden and his Tallibanis were hiding in the caves of Afghanistan.

Ullug thought that since Mulla Maqsood is here his task should be easy.

"Ullug! You get fresh. I will go to the store and I will help my daddy in closing it. More over it is already evening time, I will come back from the store and we will take dinner together. I have talked about you to my daddy. He is keen to meet you."

As Rushdi left, Ullug once again looked at the packet and started thinking that how this virus filled packet can be sent to Miami?. But before that he has to go to the lab, where he can revive the life of dry cells kept in this packet.

Fahad Mallik kept on looking at Ullug. Rushdi introduced "Abba! He is my friend Ullug, Ullug Beg."

"From your name it appears that you are from Uzbekistan."

Ullug looked at Fahad with a great surprise. He thought if one can know the place to which someone belongs to just from the name, then that man must be very clever.

"Sir—chachajaan! Salam Alekum!" Ullug said to Fahad.

Fahad liked sweetness in the tone of Ullug. His eyes were sharp and deep as if sea currents were flowing therein. How much depth must be in his sea like mind!

"What are you doing Mr. Ullug?"

"Uncle—chachajaan! Please don't call me with respect. I am just like your son Rushdi and I am of his age."

Fahad liked this politeness of Ullug. Even then why was he feeling that there was an unpleasant mask on his face?. Fahad had same feelings which he had when he met Mulla Maqsood. Will there be any kind of relation or connection between them.?

Fahad had not liked Maqsood's presence. He felt that in name of Jehad, he was doing unholy war.

"Walekum Salam! Have you come to St. Thomas for some specific purpose?"

Ullug's hand stopped while eating. Why he felt holiness of his father? Did Mr. Fahad have some suspicion for Ullug, or is it his nature?

"Uncle! i am interested in diamond business. In fact I am head of one research center in Kabul. In that context I and Rushdi met in Africa."

"Oh Rushdi! by the way, Whether your Dr. wellingodon has come out with any findings on samples collected by him?."

"Yes Abbajaan! After examining samples his report was sent to America for further process. But I am not aware about contents of the report."

"Oh Ullug! You are also in research isn't it? Recently there were news in newspapers that in the South East corner of Turkey some two to three thousand people along with children died unusually. First it was thought that it may be due to food poisoning but the latest report received from America is mentioning that it was due to specific virus which have caused their deaths."

Ullug froze and then said,

"Is it so? I was traveling so I do not know."

"Report conveys that if sudden deaths take place on account of virus then such things can happen only if some unknown person or a guest who has come to that place have brought some infection with him".He looked intently at Ullug.

There was a spark in Ullug's eyes which did not go unnoticed from Fahad.

Ullug composing himself said. "Uncle! You are well informed about world affairs."

"My son! When someone is staying alone on an island, then his mind is to be kept busy in some activity."

"Oh! There is nothing in your plate" said Rushdi's mother, saying this she kept one piece of bread in Ullug's plate. The topic was changed, but Ullug did appreciate Fahad's cleverness. In the meantime Fahad asked Rushdi. "Rushdi! Mulla Maqsood is still here or has he gone back?"

"Abbajaan! He is still here. Yesterday I took him to see our mountains and caves."

"You did not do a right thing my son."

"Why? Any tourist coming here do go to see these places."

"Yes! But I think he has come here with some other purpose."

"What purpose daddy—Abbajaan?

"Did you inquire from where has he come?"

"Yes Abba! He was telling that he is from Afghanistan. He likes mountain ranges, and so he wanted to see our mountains."

"My son! You are still not fully grown up, when he came to my office he talked about Jehad and asked for the help."

"Abbu! Jehad is a religious war and so we must help them."

"Rushdi! You are an American citizen. If someone tells you to betray, will you do it? And what is a religious war?."

"Abbu!" Rushdi looked confused.

"Uncle! I will give you reply, Jehad is a war against tyranny and injustice done to you."

"But before that, you should know who has done injustice and why? And for that why the whole world should be punished?. Govt. has made the law isn't it?? Should you not obey that law?".

"Abba! You are right, but Mulla Maqsood has said America is the enemy of entire Islamic world."

"No my son! Not of the entire Islamic world but of militants and terrorists who for their self interest kill innocent people. Allah will never forgive them and one should not help such people. I feel that Mulla Maqsood is a militant, please keep away from him."

"Uncle! He is traveling to all countries. He is asking help for religion. can you refuse him.?"

"My son! It is fine for the religion but not for the person who spreads terrorism. And you told about his traveling? I remember one dialogue of Al-Mustafa who was an eternal traveler."

"I am an ongoing traveler on the sea shores. Sand is spread all over, ocean foams spread everywhere. My foot steps are on the sand. waves of tide will wash them away, along with my foot steps. But the roaring ocean will remain here for ever, sea shore will remain here for ever. My son! Ocean is our life and we the human beings are it's shores. Everybody should know relationship between the ocean and its shores. Ullug, come to my store tomorrow." After Dinner was over, Rushdi went with Ullug in his room.

After both of them left the room Fahad said to his wife "Farida Begum—wife!". We are staying here peacefully but this Mulla Maqsood appears to be a s torm and I foresee same thing in Ullug. Please be on guard and take care that our son Rushdi is not be trapped in that. We have only one son."

CHAPTER 13

It was early morning, mild flow of wind passing through the window came from the hills and had a mild touch on Ullug's face. Giving body a stretch and shaking off idleness, Ullug got up and stood near window.

He kept on seeing that rocky mountain. so nigh as if touching the sky! In Ullug's mind his father's philosophy poured out,. "these mountain touching sky like an ambitions of human being, caves in the mountain like caves in human mind, silence and peace in those caves but human mind is always turbulent. The silky touch of this breeze is like Farhana's hand. Everything was transparent and pious. The hills and the Sun give warmth. Moon with moonlight spreads on green grass, courting each other.so peaceful it was you can hear your own breath, but human mind is ever so restless!

In the ocean like mind of Ullug again heard the voice of the storm. As if he was surrounded by worldly temptations. He thought about activities to be done. He became active. He took bath. He offered prayers— Namaz. He had already removed his beard and mustache. Now he looked like an European guy. He opened the diamond packet, he took out virus filled syringe.

Everything was frozen in ice. He got ready to go to the lab and went down for breakfast.

Other family members were waiting for him on the breakfast table. Fahad, has heard the conversation of Ullug and Rushdie. He took a seat on the table and said "Rushdi Ullug? What is today's program?"

Abba! Ullug wants to see my lab. After seeing that, I will come to the store and after lunch I will take him to the mountain. Ullug wants to go to Miami in two to three days.

"Miami! You were supposed to go to Kabul? "uncle!" since I have already come upto here then I will visit a new place like Miami and from there a direct flight i can get. It will be easy."

"After giving some thought Fahad said" Hum! Ullug you are the only son of your daddy—Abba? Isn't it?

"Yes uncle! He got killed in American, Afghanistan War" Ullug's voice trembled with emotion.

"son!' you know that how much dear is the only son to his father? Rushdi is also my only son. He is straight forward so I have to be careful and see that he does not go off the track."

"Yes uncle! Yesterday night only I discussed same things with him and made him understand" And Ullug looked down. He could not dare to look at Fahad."

"Good! Your made him understand everything but do you understand everything?

"Uncle! I have given away my life to Jehad. After reaching Kabul via Miami i will look forward for the new situations over there"

"And are you sure you will go to to Kabul from Miami?"

"Ullug stammered as he was lying but said Yes! Yes!"

Saying "OK" everybody got up.

In the car. Rushdi said "Ullug!. Please let me accompany you.

"No! You heard what uncle has said. He needs you very much. I know my destiny." HE said with a sad voice.

"Ullug! Do you want to book a ticket to go to Miami?"

"I need your help in that matter. After two days my packet is to be sent to Mr. Ajmel Kureshi, in Miami. I will give you his address. Now tell me by which other route you can safely go to Miami?"

"One cruise is leaving from hear for Miami. Tourist take its advantage. It is a pleasant and enjoyable journey."

"Then let us go to Marina Dock and inquire on which day the cruise sails."

Both of them went to Marina Dock and on inquiring they came to know that this cruise is after three days. Another one was after two weeks. Everything was happening as per Ullug's plans. His lab work will be over in three days. Then they booked the ticket and started together for the lab. Ullug kept on seeing the capital city of St. Thomas. It was full of richness and with tourists. In the "Downtown" area in the middle of the city, on the main street there were numerous stores. All the Asians were having their stores on this road. Even in day time, the jewelery stores and garment stores were very well lighted. Hindu, Muslim and African people were staying amicably.

There was only one college in Emily. The car entered in its campus. There was greenery all around. Students were moving around.

"Rushdi! These students must be going to u.s.a. for further study?"

"Yes! There is a sizable difference in fee structure/"

"Then why you went to England?"

"Daddy was of the opinion that study in England is the best."

Both of them reached at that lab building. Ullug seeing the facilities over there was impressed He went to Rushdi's area of operation. Rashdi said "Ullug! nobody will disturb you. you can work peacefully. On this side there is Incubation Room. Once you finish the work please lock everything. This is my room. Incubation is my personal division I am going to the store. This is the telephone number of the store. Please call me once you finish you work here".

"Rushdi! You wanted to accompany in my jehad so, in directly you are doing so. I will have to use you Incubation room for two days."

"Certainly you can make the use. Can I ask you a question why you need it?."

"Rushdi!I don't want to involve you in this matter. Yes but when are we meeting Mulla Maqsood?" Your presence is not required then.

"Ullug! You are becoming more mysterious, why it is so?"

"Rushdi! I have given a promise to uncle so you have to keep away."

"OK Ullug! in the afternoon, while picking him up we will go towards mountains."

"You go away, after dropping us there. Please arrange one mobile phone for me for three days. So I can talk to you if needed. Saying "OK" Rushdi left."

Ullug closed the door of the research room and took out syringes and kept there on a table. He started the incubator and kept the temperature at the degree required to activate virus. The virus after getting activated in two days can be used on any one. Parcel will go by air to Miami, and he will go by cruise so nobody will have any doubt.

In this task Rushdi, Fahad and Ajmel Kureshi may get caught! "then? With this thought he got a shiver. But these was no other alternative but face the destruction. It' took about two hours to arrange various things. He came out of the incubator room locked the room and, he came to Rushdi's Office and called. "hello"

"I am Fahad Mallik?" May i help you?

"Uncle! I am Ullug. Will you please give the phone to Rushdi?"

Seeing the number of Rushdi research lab on the caller ID, Fahad Mallik got surprised. What Ullug must be doing alone in the lab?

"Yes I am giving" Saying this he gave the phone to Rushdi. He started thinking deeply."

"Rushdi! Your phone?"

Rushdi took the phone "Yes! I am coming." Saying this he turned to Fahad. "Daddy—Abba! We will take our meals in the town. From there I will take him o the mountain. I will come back in time."

Rushdi started leaving the store. looking at the back of Rushdi a worried look came to his face.

"Rushdi telephoned Ullug who was in the lab." I am bringing Mulla, Maqsood along with me. You lock the lab and take care of the keys. Your wait at campus gates, we are coming."

The car stopped at Mulla Maqsood's hotel. Looking the changed appearance of Mulla Maqsood. Rushdi was surprised.

There was a drastic change in him then the first time. At that time he was looking like an out law, with a covered face, turban on head a pathani dress looking like a militant and now clean shaved man looking handsome like an English man wearing jeans & T-Shirt? Rushdi could not recognize him at first sight. If Mulla Maqsood would not had called him from reception counter. Rushdi would not have found him.

"Hi! Rushdi" Rushdi was inquiring about him at reception counter, he turned back and replied." 'Hi' and he turned to Reception Counter.

"Rushdi! No need of asking. The person about whom you are inquiring is standing in front of you. You cannot remember my voice?"

"Oh" Seeing with surprise Rushdi said, You are completely . . . ."

"Sh—! Don't say anything any further. Any one may listen."

"But . . . ."

"Say Maqsood only"

"But you in this attire?"

"This people must feet that I am a tourist. My dress reveals my identity. You know that after 9\ 11 the surveillance is very tight."

"But does the religion approve you to do such a thing?"

Saying this and holding his hand Maqsood took Rushdi out. and said," All country people are trained in America. Their eyes and ears are very sharp.

"One has to follow according to the time and circumstances. Moreover be a Roman in Rome. Your friend, what is his name?"

"Ullug Beg!"

"When are we going to meet!"

"Just now"

"How is your daddy? He did not like my presence."

"My daddy is simple religion minded person. He is good and his business is good."

"Do you thinck so? I feel that he knows of world events, more than any body else."

"Maqsood! He is fond of CNN and BBC News. He also watches Indian and pakistani channels so is well aware of news of those countries. He should have some activity on this small island to keep himself busy."

"Rushdi a Muslim, forgets everything once they go to foreign country. They forget Muslim people, they forget religion and Jehad. That is why we travel to different countries and perform our duty to make a Union of Islam religion. Ok forget everything, when have we to go to meet your friend?"

At college gate.He wanted to see my research lab and he had some work over there. So leaving him there, I went to the store."

"Did he tell you what work he had in the lab?"

"He had some work in context to the research center."

Hearing this, Maqsood's eyes became deadly poisonous, but he composed himself before it can reflect or his face.

"After that where are we going?"

"Brother Maqsood. He wants to see the mountains and the caves. I will leave both of you there for two three hours! I will go to the store to help my father. You ring me up when you finish your task. I will come to pick you up again."

"And Rushdi do not tell to your daddy about my meeting with your friend."

Unnecessarily he will be disturbed. At this age he needs some mental rest also. you please look after him properly.

Maqsood had learned. American manners, dress code, the state of working and talking. His mind was busy in planning what is to be discussed with Ullug. college campus came. Ullug was there at the gate. He was also looking like an American. Instead greeting in a traditional way they said HI to each other. All took seats in car.

Rushdi introduced each other. Poor Rushdi was not aware about the fact that both knew each other for sometime right from Kabul.

Slowly car was moving up on the hilly road. Ullug and Maqsood were talking casually looking the beauty of mountain. There were lots of tourists. There was a small cafe and small shops to attract the tourists. Rushdie said "Ullug keep this cell phone. You ring me up and I will come and pick you up. Tomorrow we will go to one famous resort".

Ullug and Maqsood proceeded toward cafe.

"Let us have coffee" Maqsood was knowing that American are very much fond of coffee." While working even they—Americans have a coffee mug in their hands. Both took the seat. Maqsood asked "Ullug! what about your mission?"

"You don't know?"

"What?"

"What happened in the Caspian Sea on the North-Eastern park of Turkey?"

"Yes! I have heard the news about that event"

"You might also heard the news that America wants to invade on Iraq—on Sadaam?"

"Yes! But still I could not understand the context."

"Why he wants to invade?"

"For two reasons. One excuse is that Sadaam has colleted chemical weapons for Mass Destruction. Do you remember he has massacred millions of Kurd people with nuero Chemical gas? Now he wants to invade Kuweit, Jr. Bush wants to complete unfinished work of Sr. Bush."

"Why you use the word excuse?"

"I feel it is an excuse. America is getting ready for invasion to take revenge. So long as I believe Sadaam does not have that type of ammunition."

"Then why Sadaam does not allow U.N. team to survey the situation?"

"Because his ego might hurt."

"Yes! But what relation this matter has with Turkey incident?"

"Maqsood Miya do you know that I have met Osama Bin Laden in Kabul?"

"Yes! But . . . ."

"He knows about my African visit of Russian research center."

"So what!"

"From there we brought samples of virus of chimpanzees. They also know about killer virus."

"Yes but what is the purpose!"

"Still you are not in a position to understand? It is alleged that Sadaam wants to use chemical warfare. With this virus Osama Bin Laden wants to have "Bio

Terrorism" a biological warfare against America. This is also one type of Jehad. I am ready to be useful for that."

"In what way?"

"Before other tourtsts become suspicious let us go to see the caves. We will talk more about this in there.

Both of them got up and joined one group of tourists. While moving forward in the caves, an open place came. A holy looking person was giving a kind of a lecture.

Hearing the name of Gibran. Ullug and Maqsood stopped. That saintly man cited. "How many of you know the name of Gibran?," Few people raised their hands. Do you know the place where he was born?" In a small village near Lebanon, Syria. He narrated one funny but interesting incident. Gibran was staying in New York. One American went to Syria as a tourist. There he asked one Syria citizen.

"Do you know Gibran? The man asked in return a question" Do you know Shakespeare?. That America said that the whole world knows him."

You got your answer. said the Syrian.

"In middle East even children know about him."

One tourist raising his hand said "Will you tell us in brief something about him?"

"Listen! Said Gibran" I move in search of truth, my traveling soul experience small pleasures in this world while traveling. MY world becomes small but my head remains high.I produce independent thinking when it is high.If you think small, you will remain small. Think high you will become ambitious.Expand your vision. Take this small book at a nominal price and read one incident before you go to sleep. you will get your destination."

"Ullug and Maqsood looked at each other hearing this philosophy of life. There was a deep meaning hidden in it. They proceeded further."

"Ullug! Tell me how are you going to help? We will talk while walking."

"I have a secrete plan. Tell me from here where will you go?"

"I will go to Kabul via Miami."

"I will reach Miami in two days time taking a cruise from here. You also come and join the cruise. We can reach without any disturbance there. And you can take my message to Osama."

"OK! We will have to book tickets."

"I will call Rushdi. But before he arrives,. we will go to Marina to buy the tickets then, he leaving you at your hotel I will go with Rushdi. He will take us at Marina dock on the day of departure."

They came out of the caves and Ullug called Rushdi.

CHAPTER 14

Rushdi came.

Along with Mulla Maqsood, Ullug and Rushdi went to Marina Docks and bought tickets of the cruise.

"Ullug! It's good that you will have company of Mulla Maqsood and voyage of cruise is also very interesting. How nice would it be if I could have come with you?"

Before Maqsood could say anything Ullug said "Rushdi your father needs you here" Maqsood did not say anything.

While dropping Maqsood at his hotel, Ullug said "Be ready tomorrow".

On Maqsood's getting out of the car, Ullug said "Rushdi will you drop me at your lab? I have two / three hours work over there. I must finish my work today. I will close your lab and after dropping uncle at home will you please come and collect me? Do you have any objection?"

Rushdie said "No! Ullug! But shall I tell you one thing why don't you allow me to accompany you in your Jehad".

"Rushdi! You are only twenty four years old and only son of your parents. He needs you. At the time when my daddy wanted me at that time I was not with him even at his death bed. I am grieved by it. A person knows value of things that he has missed."

Ullug got down at the lab. Today he has taken his back pack. He entered the lab and locking the room, he went to Incubation Room. All syringes were activated. One prick and the show will be over. He collected activated eggs from incubation dishes and kept the same along with syringes in an ice pad. He made them to freeze and kept everything in his back pack. He finished his work in two hours. Thinking that now the destination is not far off, he telephoned to Rushdi.

"Destination? Where is it? What does it contain?" Ullug kept on thinking. But to reach to the goal he was prepared to sacrifice his life.

As Rushdi came, Ullug took his seat in the car and asked "Rushdi! Did you drop uncle at home? Did he ask you anything?"

"Yes! He was asking where you went after seeing the mountains?"

"I told him that you went to the lab".

"Did he say anything?"

After a pause he said, "What work can he have in your lab?"

"I had to say that to send some information about his research to Kabul he has gone to the lab."

"Rushdi! Uncle looks aged but mentally he is more alert than all of us."

Both of them reached home. As per trend in America, people take biting in afternoon and take full dinner between 6 to 7 p.m. Ullug went to his room. Keeping his back pack, and after getting fresh, he came down. All took their seats on the dining table. For sometime, Fahad Mallick kept on looking at Ullug. He was sad as he was thinking that in name of Jehad, how young talents go wasted and said "Ullug! Rushdi has said that you are going to Miami and from there you will take a flight for Kabul is it so?."

"Yes uncle—chachajaan! I want to go to Kabul at the earliest. I have to complete my father's after death ceremony" Ullug said with tears in his eyes.

"Ullug! My son!" Fahad's voice was full of emotions. "What type of assignments you had undertaken so that you could not attend your father's funeral?"

"Uncle—chachajaan! I am in this Jehad against the injustice done to me"

"Do you really believe that injustice has been done to you? Can it be not called just an accident? You told that Farhana's death has been caused by one American soldier. But people of our own community do not rape women?"

"My father also died at hands of Americans. Is it not injustice?".

"Many situations come up during a war. I am not saying this because. I am an American Citizen, but all happenings should be fully analyzed. You felt that injustice has been done to you but same cannot be just an echo of injustice done to someone else also?".

"But Uncle! When that echo breaks your heart then what will you do?"

"My son! Prophet Mohammed has said in Holy Book of Koran to forgive misdeeds of others. Even then if you want to take revenge, it should be with persons who had done injustice to you. But for that, in name of Jehad, you cannot kill the whole community and innocent people."

Ullug got stunned but said "Uncle! American Govt. has punished that soldier in Court Martial in this matter, but, our Muslim brothers are being killed in our country what about that?"

To call Americans in homeland is justified as per military law of this country. Afghan rulers are responsible for their soldiers. They are Muslims In that case they are responsible"

Ullug had never thought in that line. If it is so then why Al-Qaeda and Osama Bin Laden are instigating Muslims and Islamic world against Americans or Non-Muslims?

"Ullug! What you think is correct. There is an echo of my thoughts in your mind. Do you know Mulla Maqsood?"

With a great surprise he kept on looking at Fahad; He said. "My son! He came to me asking for help. I feel he is Al-Qaeda Militant—terrorist. Be on guard. In order to get recognition you might lose your life. I am deeply worried about you. You are just like my son".

"Uncle—chachajaan I have no regret for non-achievement of my goal. It is just a stepping stone. But when ambition overflows then one gets disturbed."

"Since you are young, you feel so. But learn to be alert and clever. You are leaving tomorrow isn't it? Rushdi was telling that you want to send your diamond packet to Miami by post so that you will not have to carry any risk."

"Yes uncle—chachajaan! He is right, I will hand over the packet to Rushdi. Uncle you and aunt have treated me like your son." While saying this, Ullug's eyes were full of tears.

Fahad kept on looking at Ullug and was thinking.

"How nice, beautiful and emotional is his soul? But in whims of Jehad he may have been trapped in immoral activities. At present organizations like Al-Qaeda and others have brainwashed minds of young men to go on suicidal way." While getting up from dinning table Fahad had a deep sigh and he went to his room.

Ullug also got up and went to his room. He opened his bag and took out back pack and kept two-three incubation dishes containing Virus in a plastic bag with syringes and kept the same hiding in between clothes. In cruise there will not be much scrutiny. Even if this post parcel gets lost even then he will have some Virus in his bag. Other dishes and syringes he kept with diamond packed the parcel and went to sleep. Fahad's advice echoed in his mind. He closed his eyes and faces of Farhana and his father came before his eyes. Again thoughts came on the surface. To day was over and he was one step forward to his destination. Today's date was off the calendar as if a leaf falls off a tree. But where does the leaf knows that so long it was on a tree, it had a support. But now having fallen down from the tree that support has gone. Now it has to depend on the flow of air and as if it has lost its independence.

"Was he dependent on Al-Qaeda?. Now there is no time to think for that matter. They are like a cobweb in our mind which once gets over, there is a full stop. New start is a fresh beginning, and with that end in also linked". He got up from his bed and thought of an end. Why that thought came in his mind?. He has prepared himself for a sacrifice for cause of Jehad, which will also have an end one day or the other.

Leaving all turmoil of thoughts, he slept with a disturbed mind. If daddy—Abba would have been alive would he have accepted his heinous task of killing thousands of innocent people through these Virus? With great effort he tried to sleep.

Fahad Mallik was in a dilemma. "Shall he call? What to do? By doing so will there not be any injustice?".

He also slept with a disturbed mind.

Next day morning Fahad got up with swollen eyes. While sitting on dining table he said "Dear Ullug! Listen! Please go with due care".

"Yes uncle—chachajaan."

Ullug got up from his seat and embraced Fahad Mallick. He felt as if he is leaving a part of his heart behind. Fahad said "Good Bye—Khuda Hafeez".

While seating in car, Rushdi said "Ullug you have heard what my daddy told you 'Good Bye'. Did you understand it's silent meaning?" Good Bye means there is a hope of meeting again. Daddy loves you as his son."

After seeing off Mulla Maqsood and Ullug, Rushdi went to pick up his father to take him to the store.

Fahad Mallick went to his room stared at the phone. He thought "What shall I do!"

Chief of Homeland Securities, Mr. Christie asked "Zeba! Do you want to go to Turkey?. Tissues received from there, are getting examined. Agreeing to the request from Turkey Govt., you have to go there to find out who has spread killing viruses? Will you go?"

Zeba was ready to accept any challenge. After talking with Shekhar she left for Ankara along with her FBI team. In the flight she was thinking when her mission will get over and when can she get united with Shekhar?" Her treasure of love, its fragrance is yet to blossom. she had just felt soft touch of it like a soft breeze!

Many times she was thinking that Shekhar was a research expert and being a South Indian, he was well versed in Southern music and literature. His mother was a poet and she was writing good poems, in front of Zeba, he read one poem with meanings. The poem was quite refreshing and full of feelings touching her heart.

No, No, not to be hated,
Man is worth loving,
Though having faults,
Human being is worth,
To be sung in poems
At the end a man
Is worth loving.

Shekhar was worth loving. His parents were a Brahmin family from Southern India—an orthodox family, then will they permit their son to marry a Muslim? What is there if I am a Muslim? They believe in God. I also believe in Khuda our God. Words for prayers are different but meaning is the same. Suppose I change my name and keep a Hindu name will it bring a change in my life style to that of a Hindu girl? Then can I be called Hindu? Fine, what is religion? Is the family in which you are born or your religion is from your deeds and action?. After all one's duty rightly performed is religion. Then what is there in being a Hindu, a Muslim or a Christian? Only difference is the way in which one prays.

Mission for which she is going is to find out a person who had spread Virus. Who will he be? To which community he must be belonging to? Due to few terrorists entire community is blamed.

Her name is Zeba Khalid. If she does not have a FBI badge then she would also be looked upon with suspicion. Findings are that due to food poisoning deaths took place, which is not the fact as deaths took place because of killer virus. Who must have found them? From where they were brought? Despite the security if they reach to Pentagon then how clever these terrorists must be? What is their plans? Are they fighting for Jehad or religious war?.

Is Jehad their goal to rule over the world?

She was in deep thoughts but she became conscious as her flight reached Ankara. But still she has to go to Arzuram from the hilly tracks by jeep from Ankara.

In South East corner of Turkey there is less population. It is the desert area and camel is the only vehicle. Who must have gone in such an area? Will there be a plan to experiment virus in this area of less population?.

She got down on the airport with her team of four members. From there they went to a hotel and after getting freshened up she got ready for a meeting with American Ambassador and Defense Minister of Turkey.

She reached to the Embassy Office which was having tight security around the Embassy building. Terrorists have attacked American Embassies in other countries. So security arrangements were full proof. More over Turkey was a Muslim country.

American Ambassador said. "Miss. Khalid will you please tell us about findings of the lab at your end?"

Zeba turned towards Mr. Pasha, the Defense Minister of Turkey and said "Sir these viruses are called Ebola. It is a killer virus and is known as "Ebola", Saying this she showed photographs of the virus.

Their photographs were magnified. They are like very small snakes and they grow once they enter human body. Symptoms like vomiting, stomach pain, cough, cold and fever as well as, blood in stools take place. Body goes weak and dehydration takes place.

Irrespective of medicine, affected persons meet their deaths in three day's time.

"Right. you gave a correct picture. On festival day in Arzuram after dinner people died on third day."

"Sir! There is very strict security in Ankara. Arzuram is very far off from Ankara. To reach that particular place is quite difficult in desert area. It is not case of Turkey only. In North-Eastern part of Turkey to get away from Sadaam Hussain the Kurds were staying there doing business of cattle farming".

"Do you think that someone might have entered from Iraq?"

"Sadaam Hussain has killed many Kurds through chemical gas, to wipe out Kurds from this region. It is quite possible that some one might have been sent."

"Through which other route can you reach Arzuram?"

"You can reach from Azerbaijan Port on Caspian Sea. But it is a sandy region and camel is the only transport to reach here."

"Do you think that someone might have come through that route?"

"That route is long and difficult one. Who can be interested in such a route?"

"Which are the countries surrounding Caspian Sea to reach to Port Azerbaijan?"

"A direct train is coming from Russia".

Zeba's eyes sparkled "How are political relations between Turkey and Russia?"

"Good! Normal. Do you think that politics is involved in this case?"

"Quite possible, what do you think.?

"Can there be a terrorist?"

"Is anyone entering in your boundaries—borders properly checked? Before anyone enters in your area are there any Immigration and Customs formalities?" Zeba inquired.

"Yes! All these formalities are observed."

"Any records"?

"All paper work is in respective departments."

"Are arrangements made for our team to go there.?"

"Yes! You will cover that distance by train and thereafter by camel in desert region."

"Good! We will have a new experience."

Train Journey was comfortable but when they had to ride on a back of a camel, they found it quite difficult. Zeba had never taken a camel ride. With great difficulty she could take a seat on the camel.

She almost fell when her camel got up. She would have fallen down if she had not hold the handles. She climbed on the camel with help of it's driver. Camel driver had a laugh to see her state of affairs.

"Why are you laughing? Asked Zeba".

"Similar difficulties were envisaged by my brother when he had one passenger."

"You told one passenger? Who was he?"

"Looked like a Muslim"

"From his face or dress code?"

"In both ways."

"Can you describe him little more?"

"He was a tall, stout, young man with beard and mustache wearing turban and had quite a fair look".

"Can I get his photograph?"

"Madam! Quite a few travelers come and go. Many photographs are taken. On reaching Arzuram. I will search for it at my residence."

Gradually with great difficulty, and they reached to Arzuram.

Population at Arzuram had almost died. Only those people who did not participate in that festival were alive. No clue was available from them. While inquiring with immigration people it was known that many passengers have arrived. No fix date of arrival is available, then how to separate the terrorist?. Zeba was confused. she asked," when was the festival. what date?

when she got the date she asked for travelers name cards. A list was prepared. There were many names, how to find that terrorist? Fortunately, when she came out in the town she met the camel driver.

"Madam! Your are really lucky. On that day my brother had only one passenger. In order to keep his memory, one photograph is taken. He also came to festival along with my brother and on the next day, he left from here."

"Was he there when affected people were being admitted in the hospital?"

"Yes! On the same evening he left for Ankara and this is his photo."

Zeba kept on staring at the picture. He was looking like a terrorist! Who can he be?".

CHAPTER 15

Ullug and Maqsood went to their cabin which was a two seater and well furnished cabin. Leaving luggage over there they went to upper deck. Still there was some time for ship to sail. Both of them looked at seashore where people were waiting to bid farewell to their friends and relatives. Ullug and Maqsood said good bye to Rushdi.

Mulla Maqsood asked "Ullug! You know Rushdi for quite some time now, and, you have also stayed with him. How did you find Fahad Mallick?."

"He is a very religious minded person. He is like my Daddy" Said Ullug.

"That is why he could not get along well with me. He feels movement of Jehad we joined is not good." said Maqsood.

Ullug. "That is his opinion."

"Is he suspicious about you?" Asked Maqsood.

"No! He has not said anything to me. I do not know if he has said anything to Rushdi about me."

"Rushdi is a young man. He can very well join with us."

"But Fahad uncle will not allow that."

"If Mr. Fahad is not there then?"

Ullug got stunned and said "No! No! Maqsood! I do not think that we should go to that extent."

Saying "Hum" Maqsood thought for a while and asked "Where are you going from Miami?"

Ullug's face became cruel but he did not reply.

As ship started sailing, both of them took their seats on it's deck. Maqsood took out some paper from his pocket and told "Ullug! You are now well aware of situation in Kabul. Now Talibanis are friends. Al-Qaeda has spread everywhere. With help of units of Pakistani army and Lashkar-e-Toiba, Talibanis have entered Pakistan Owned Kashmir. After finishing your work here, Osama wants you to join our organisation."

"I will think later on."

"Do you know where else Jehad has spread?. There is a mention about Jehad even in media."

"Shortly Jehad of Kashmir will spread in whole of Asia and we will activate Jehad in India."

"In 1996, news were flashed in Lahore Press Club, please read this press clip."

"Maqsood why Jehad movement has been raised against India.?"

"There is on going suppression of Muslims in Kashmir. How can we tolerate suppression by Indians on our brothers? You may not be knowing that in due course of time Junagadh and Hyderabad will be merged with Pakistan and Prof. Hafiz Mohd Sayed, head of Lashkar-e-Toiba is taking care of it."

"In what way?" asked Ullug.

Maqsood said "Prof. Hafiz has got good support both from Generals of Pakistani Army and I.S.I. He is staying in a posh bungalow in Lahore business area and he has constructed one mosque in his compound. He is most wanted person in India and America. He, with help of Sheikh Abu Abdel Aziz of Al-Qaeda as well as with help of. Mr. Zakir Ur Rehman Lakvy, a Senior Officer in Pakistani Army have made Union of Lashkar-e-Toiba. He is the one who is poisoning minds of young people of Kashmir for Jehad. Today more then 10,000 young people are with him."

"If whole world is considering him most wanted person then why is he not arrested?" asked Ullug.

"He is a distant family member of Mr. Nawaz Sharif, Ex-Prime Minister of Pakistan. He spends lot of money in Gulf countries. He is very popular over there as he is donating millions of Dollars."

"What are their activities?"

"They are preparing suicide squads to infiltrate in India."

"Suicide squads?"

"Yes! There are two types of suicide squads. Jana-E-Fidai and IBN-E-Imiha. In first category, suicidors are those people who sacrifice their lives out of their own will. While in second category, there are people who are suffering from incurable deceases and they do not want to live any more as they know that they are going to die soon. Willingly they get ready in name of Jehad to be a live bomb".

"Where are their training camps?"

"There are forty training camps in Pakistan Occupied Kashmi and in swat valley. They are also in places like, Afghanistan, Kajikistan, Tajikistan etc. They have infiltrate right into Muslims of Chechenya."

"It is surprising to know about their training. Moreover they should be committed to become a live bomb."

"First step of training is that they must learn foreign language of the place where they have to go. Other training is that of commandos. You may not be aware that these Talibanis are product of America only.

"How?" Ullug got surprised.

Afghanistan wanted to drive Russians out from their country. One crash training program was prepared to train Pakistani Muzahudins by C.I.A. for guerilla war, they became Talibanis and are using same tactics against America.

"It was necessary." Said Ullug with all animosity.

But Maqsood suddenly pressed Ullug's hand and made a sign to remain quiet. Their cruise had almost reached in middle of the sea. Near opposite railing, one African was standing. While talking, Maqsood was looking all around. He felt that African's movements were mysterious. Slowly Maqsood got up and went near to that African. While talking to him, he came to know that he was a Muslim from Somalia. Recently he was in Yemen. He said he went there for some training, but he did not say anything more.

Maqsood knew that there are training camps of Al-Qaeda in Yemen. He must have been trained there. But what could be his purpose to come on this cruise? In order to ensure that he does not become suspicious, Maqsood came back to Ullug's table. Seeing him deeply engrossed in thoughts, Ullug asked "What is the matter? You are in deep thoughts since you have returned after meeting him."

In the meantime, there was a dinner time bell. Cruise ship passengers entered in a posh and modern dining room. Due to many customers cruise ships were gorgeous and lavish. Dinning room was quite large. There was a live band music. Some couples were dancing on dance floor, Ullug and Maqsood came in and took their seats in front of dinning table. Ullug wanted to ask something to Maqsood but in the meantime that somalian fellow came there. He looked around and took a seat in one far off corner. Maqsood and Ullug both of them saw that Somalian. Maqsood said in a low voice.

"Ullug! I feel that, that somalian's behavior is weird".

"Why? Do you feel something odd?"

"Yes! I have an intuition that his motives are not good."

"It is good if he is a militant—terrorist. These white people will get a lesson."

"But Ullug! As good things get destroyed with bad things we might get killed."

"We are ready to die."

"Yes! But our mission is still incomplete. I have yet to complete my assignment and you also have some plans. Isn't it?"

"So?" Asked Ullug.

"We have to keep a watch on his movements" In the meantime, one lady came and asked that somalian, "May I dance with you?."

Both of them got up. Slow waltz music was on. There was a candle light on every table. Atmosphere was full of love. Young couples looking eye to eye were engrossed in sweet nothings. Even elderly people became young forgetting their stress and tension. On dance floor, couples were dancing with small steps while keeping close to their partners.

Maqsood kept on looking at that somalian. In the meantime, that somalian drew his partner closer to him. Her eyes went on his waist. Something sharp pierced on her stomach from his Jacket. His coat got opened and while seeing his waist, she screamed. His waist portion was all covered with grenades. She screamed "Oh! There is a live bomb." As Ullug and Maqsood were seating very close by, they heard the scream. Others were deeply engrossed in music so they did not hear her scream. That lady went away from him and quickly left dance floor, and that somalian also rushed out of the room. Jumping like a wild animal, Maqsood ran after him. All people saw that lady was screaming. Before security people came, people gathered on the deck.

While running, somalian reached at the railing and turned to people with remote in his hand. Maqsood understood his motive. He increased his speed and fell on that somalian. Before he could understand what is happening, Maqsood gave a big push to him and he fell in the sea. Incidentally by push, remote got pressed. One huge fire ball came out from the sea. somalian died but the cruise and passengers were saved. Seeing this, people of the ship got stunned. Later on people greeted Maqsood with large applause. Many cameras were flashed. In the meantime, Ullug stood by Maqsood to give him a support so that he may not fall down. Both of them were flashed in cameras. By that time, security people came and told people to go back to dining room.

Head of security team and captain of the ship came and there was a big celebration. Maqsood was called on the podium and he was given a big reception to save the ship and people. People were thinking that Ullug and Maqsood were looking like Americans in T-shirts and jeans and so the captain said "How courageous these Americans are?" Ullug was getting angry within him.

Once everything was quiet both of them came to their cabin. Ullug said. "Oh! You have become a hero. All these news will be flashed tomorrow in media."

"Let it be! By tomorrow we will be in Maimi. Before tomorrow's media coverage, we will be already out on our mission away from Miami."

"Maqsood! Both us do not know each other's mission, will you please tell me what is your mission.?"

"You have also not told me anything about your mission" Said Maqsood.

"By now you know that I am right hand of Osama Bin Laden of Al-Qaeda. My mission is to involve young Muslims from England and America in Jehad movement. I have failed in case of Rushdi, but does not matter. From Miami I am going to Australia, New Zealand and Fiji Islands and from there I will be going to Indonesia and Malaysia. There is a large population of Muslims over there. Now you tell me about your mission."

"Sadaam Hussein had massacred the Kurds through Neuro chemical weapons. Through Biological warfare I am going to destroy Washington D.C. Osama knows about my plans."

"Very good! Where are you going to stay in Miami?"

"At one of our Muslim brother's place. Without knowing much about me he is helping me. Where are you going to stay?".

"In a Hotel, Someone's contact may put you in trouble. Please be cautious." Thinking about future both of them went to sleep.

Suddenly Maqsood asked Ullug "Ullug your name is uncommon, what does it mean?.

"Setting Sun" said ullug.

"Will Sun of Ullug also set?". Thinking this Maqsood went to sleep.

It was a morning time Ullug was ready to start but his face was gloomy. His mind was disturbed. He was just thinking. "By now parcel must have reached to Mr. Kureshi. Rushdi knew that there are diamonds in it. He was knowing people in Customs Department, so there should not be any problem. He also informed Mr. Kureshi at Miami, so there should not be in any problem for him also. Even then he did not trust anyone. He was raw—novice in matter of Jehad. He was unaware of politics being played at the top. Maqsood also was not that straight forward. He should know everything as he is Osama's right hand. He must be knowing about me too and he must have talked about me to Mr. Osama. But my work is unique and independent and my Jehad is against the injustice done to me"

Maqsood also got up. After taking bath, he came out of bathroom only by wrapping one towel on his body. For the first time Ullug saw Maqsood's well built fair body. There was no beard and mustache and his face was quite bright. His Commando like well built body, broad chest, long hands, and smooth legs all these were noticed by Ullug. He just said "Maqsood! Your body is very well looked after. Where is your wife and children? Do they stay with you.?"

Maqsood got stunned but then he said with a smile, "Ullug you only told me that we are carrying our death warrant with us then where is the question of having a family.?"

"But my dear brother" said Ullug.

This very word 'brother' made Maqsood very emotional. He embraced Ullug and said "Ullug after how many years I have heard the word 'Dear brother" saying this his eyes were full of tears.

"I had a younger brother like you. During Russian—Afghan war my parents died in bomb shelling and my brother became an orphan. Talibanis gave him protection and he became a militant and in Taliban—American war my younger brother died in cross—bullet fire by my own hands."

Ullug also gave a warm response to Maqsood's hug.

"Ullug! Since you have told me dear brother, please take care. Do not under estimate FBI. They have long hands."

"Dear brother—Bhaijaan! I do not mind to be sacrificed once my mission in fulfilled then I will have no regrets."

"But suppose you are caught before that then.? You will have life time imprisonment."

"I will not allow that to happen. I am holding virus whose destination is America but I will use that Virus if I am caught."

"But if it is snatched away from you then.?"

"I will find out some way. But I will not be the victim of their oppression." There was a spark of determination on Ullug's face.

"Ullug! Is Mr. Kureshi trustworthy.?"

"He does not know anything about me. He just helps me as another Muslim."

"Even then you remain cautious" said Maqsood.

After finishing their bath, both of them went to dining room.

Captain and all members of the crew were ready to greet Maqsood with flowers in their hands. Passengers also greeted him by big clap. The cruise anchored in the docks. Ullug and Maqsood got shocked seeing assembly of media persons on the docks. Both of them thought "Now there is no option but to be flashed on T.V."

They did not know that thief always leave a sign behind.

Ajmal Kureshi came to receive them. He also insisted Maqsood to be his guest. But Maqsood said no. After giving interview to media people both of them parted.

The car started and Ajmal Kureshi said "Ullug! Your parcel had arrived from St. Thomas".

Ullug thought "After reaching home I will call Rushdi and Fahad Mallick about his safe arrival. But again he thought "Will Fahad Mallick create obstacles in my mission?".

CHAPTER 16

On reaching home Ullug found that Ajmal Kureshi's residence was quite good. One separate room was made ready for him. He got fresh and came to living room. On seeing furniture and fixtures, Ullug realized that Kureshi was quite well off.

Both Ajmal and Ullug came to dinning table. Ajmal's wife Ameena came from kitchen. Their daughter Akilla was with her. She was very beautiful and was having bright eyes. Her young face was evidencing her intellect. From other room one young man entered. Every one took their seats and food was served.

"Ullug! There are lots of praises for you and your friend in media. You saved the Cruise ship voyagers from one militant. It was a big adventure."

"Ajmal Uncle! How can we forget our duty towards humanity?" To change the topic he said "You are staying here for many years isn't it? What is your homeland?"

"Ullug! Originally we are from Hyderabad, Andhra Pradesh in India. After partition of India and Pakistan, Nizam's Hyderabad Kingdom was merged with India by Sardar Vallabhai Patel. During that time I got a chance to come to America. After coming here, I got franchise of gas station. Along with it, I started one convenient store where you get provisions. I and your sister-in-law labored like anything. We used to work from 8 a.m. to 10 p.m. God favored us and at present I have got three petrol stations and for that I have kept two managers. After birth of Akilla and Jamshed, your sister-in-law looks after domestic affairs. Both my children are well brought up.

"Dear Ullug! What are you doing? which place you belong to"? Asked Jamshed.

"Oh! You speak very good Urdu."

"Ullug! Children born here basically talk in English. But Ameena has made both of them to study Urdu at home. On every Sunday children are taught Urdu in Mosque and they have to read Holy Book of Koran. Both my children know Urdu quite well.

"Dear Jamshed! I am head of one Research laboratory in Kabul. I am originally from Tashkent, Uzbekistan which is now an independent country. It got liberated from Russia. What are you doing Jamshed?"

"I am a pilot. I am quite well off due to my Daddy's encouragement."

"I am running Montessori Day Time school" said Akilla.

"Ullug! I informed you that your parcel has arrived which I have kept in your room."

"Uncle! I have sent it with due care. Thank God it has reached safely."

"Are there some personal goods also in that parcel? Sorry I should not have asked you this question." Said Ajmal Kureshi.

Uncle! One of my Indian friends from Kabul is interested in diamonds and I have bought diamonds for him from Antwerp. I had to go to St. Thomas so I was worried about how to take care of these valuables. In the meantime, you met me, so I sent parcel at your address here."

"Good that I met you. Any relations in St. Thomas?"

"No! But I have a friend over there. His father has a jewelery and diamond store."

"What is his name?"

"Fahad Mallick."

Ajmal Kureshi and Ameena looked at each other and exchanged something without using words.

After dinner they all went to living room. Jamshed—jimmy and Akilla went to their rooms, Ajmal said. "Ullug! You mentioned Fahad Mallick. I have heard his name. How do you know him.?"

"His son Rushdi and I were studying together. Fahad Mallick is a religious minded person."

"I have heard his name. He is highly respected in Caribbean Island and he is respected even in Miami. Being of the same caste, I asked about him. Does he have any children?"

"Yes! He has one son. He has come back from London after studying in research programming. Now he is chief in one laboratory at St. Thomas University."

"What is his name?"

"His name is Rushdi."

"He must be your friend. How is he?" All of a sudden Ullug got point of Ajmal's inquiry.

Ajmal Kureshi might be thinking for Akilla to get a good match for her. In front of his eyes there was a picture of a fair and handsome Rushdi. It appears God has thought of a good couple.

"Unlce! He is quite handsome boy having very good character. He is an excellent boy."

"May I ask you one question?" Saying this Ajmal Kureshi once again looked at Ameena.

"Yes! Please do ask".

"We are looking for a match for our daughter Akilla, and we do not want to send her far away from Miami."

"Very good! It appears God has thought of a very good pair."

"Then when you talk to Mr. Fahad Mallick about having received your parcel, will you talk to him about this matter as well.?"

"Certainly, I will talk to him tomorrow only." Saying this Ullug got up and went to his room.

After going to his room he opened the parcel and found that everything was safe. Now he has to plan out about his moving out from here. He saw that there was a small fridge in his room. He opened it and kept the parcel in it. Rushdi's face came before his eyes and next to his face he saw Akilla. He had an illusion that he and Farhana are standing next to each other.

His subconscious mind got active, and he was lost in world of memories. Where are those streams which were flowing away and where are those wide spread trees? What has been left with him now? While going away after meeting Farhana, aimless loneliness was felt. How sweet was it in those days to be alone in his room?. That loneliness after meeting Faehana was so sweet while now same loneliness is bringing boredom. How great is the difference in loneliness then and loneliness now. That kind of life was giving something while this life is taking away everything. Where do I find that life?

And gradually dreaming about Farhana's face he started getting sleep.

Ajmal Kureshi and Ameena were talking in their room. "Madam—begum! What do you think? You want to find a match of American culture for Akilla or son of Fahad Mallick of St. Thomas?"

"Do you know to which place Mr. Fahad Mallick belongs to?"

"So long as I know he is from Andhra Pradesh and his town should be Hyderabad only. The way in which Ullug gave his details, it can be construed that Rushdi is under American influence and Muslim culture as well. As he has studied in England, so his cultural values must be good."

"But before we decide anything, we should ask Akilla? What if she has already someone in her life, then what?'

"You are right shall we call her?"

Ameena went to Akilla's room. She was getting ready for next day's job with her school children. She had long hair and has maintained her figure. She had put on Jeans and T-Shirt. Her face was delicate and she had sharp eyes. Her pointed chin was describing her stubborn and intelligent! nature.

"Dear Akilla!"

"Yes! Mom—Ammijaan!" She replied while continuing her work.

"Dear! Your Daddy is calling you."

Akilla looked at her mother and asked. "What is he up to today?. Has he brought some present for me?" Akilla was very much loved by her father.

"Dear Akilla. Something is like that only". Saying Ameena started smiling.

"Mom—Ammi! Today you appear to be mysterious. Come let us go".

Both of them came to Ajmal Kureshi's bed room which was quite big. One sofa set was kept opposite to the bed.

"Come! Dear! I want to ask you something".

"Daddy—Abba please do."

"Dear! We are staying here since many years. Besides being parents we are more like friends to you. There is no secret between four of us. I want to ask you something."

"Yes Dad Abba!" Akilla could not understand what was in his mind.

"Dear! Now you are grown up. Before we start looking out good match for you, we want to ask you something."

"What Dad—Abba?".

"Have you decided any one as your life partner?".

"Oh Dad—Abba! what is the hurry? Still I want to expand my school further. Why are you in so much hurry?. Is there something missing in my love towards you?"

"No Dear! But everything should happen at the right time."

Akilla got naughty. "Then daddy—Abba he can be a Hindu or an American.?"

"You understand everything and your decision will be quite worthy. you are raised with proper values of life."

"Do you trust me so much?"

"Parents must trust their children. Staying in this country we are not orthodox. But if marriage takes place in our community then it becomes easy for both the families to know each other better. You know that in younger generation little disagreement in between them and they go for divorce, and young persons get separated from their parents. Now tell me what is in your mind?'

"Daddy—Abba! The boy is Afro-American." And there was an unusual silence in the room. Ameena threw herself on sofa. It was felt that she will become unconscious. Seeing this Akilla became serious.

"Oh! Mom—Ammi! What happened?" Saying this she got up and brought one water bottle from fridge and said. I was just joking".

"is this a joke? My heart just sank." said Ameena.

"You were telling that you have full trust in me but got disturbed like this. Look I have not thought anything in this matter" said Akilla.

Hearing this, Ajmal Kureshi and Ameena both were very happy. Ajmal said "Dear Akilla, Ullug has mentioned about one good boy. He is from our community. He is son of one very famous Jeweler staying in close by Caribbean Island, St. Thomas. His name is Rushdi. He is the son of Fahad Mallick."

"Daddy—Abba! Leaving my work here will I have to go there?"

"Darling! After marriage, daughters have to go to their in laws' house".

"Can you not call him here? How to live without all of you?" Both of them laughed.

"Dear you cannot go against law of the land. More over Rushdi is only son of Fahad Mallick. He looks after family shop and he is head of one research laboratory in a college there."

"How do you know those people.?"

"We do not know them, but Ullug is going to talk to them tomorrow."

"Daddy—Abba! You trust Ullug very much."

"Dear! He is from our community and he is our guest! While talking there was a reference about Rushdi. So we thought why not to take a chance."

"Ullug is highly introvert. From his face it appears that something is bothering him or he is hiding something from us."

"Yes Dear! He was to marry one of his colleagues but one American soldier raped her. Ultimately she died. His father also was killed in Taliban War. It is because of that, he is all the time thinking something or the other. Any way it is his personal matter".

"But Daddy—Abba! Without trusting any one, you yourself go to St. Thomas and make necessary inquires".

"Dear! Who will look after store here.?"

"Daddy—Abba! Jamshed was working with you before he became a pilot and he knows this work. He can take one week vacation. He and Mom will took after the store here."

"Then shall I take it yes from your side"? Asked Ajmal Kureshi.

"But Daddy—Abba how can I say yes before I see that boy? You do one thing, you go there, meet those people and invite that boy to our place here. Thereafter it is God's wish."

Ajmal and Ameena kept on looking at their clever daughter.

Next day Ajmal told to Ullug. "Ullug please talk to Fahad Mallick and tell him about my line of thinking. I will also talk to him. What do you think?"

"Thank God! Your idea is wonderful." Saying this he called. At the other end Fahad Mallick picked up the phone.

"Salaam Alekum chachajaan! I am Ullug speaking. I want to talk to you about something pleasant."

Saying this he discussed the matter in great detail. "Uncle—chachajaan! please talk to Ajmal Uncle please talk with him. I feel Rushdi may not get a girl like Akilla. Fahad Mallick and Ajmal Kureshi talked with each other. Fahad said brother Ajmal you come over, we will talk in detail".

"Yes uncle! what did he say?"

"He has invited me there."

"You must go there and there are many other people from our community. You can also look someone for Jamshed."

Jamshed laughed and said "Ullug as if you have come here to buy and sell diamonds."

"Our elders always talk like this and say, my son is like a diamond, and my daughter is like a jewel. Isn't it uncle.?"

"Yes Ullug! If this good work is getting done by you we will never forget you."

"Ajmal uncle! tomorrow I want to go to Washington D.C. but not by air. Is there any other mode of transport?."

"Ullug! You have come here for the first time so you do not want to see country side? One Sun Shine Express train is going to Washington D.C. from Miami. Journey is long but you will enjoy."

"For that what I shall have to do?"

"Nothing! I have taken one week leave from tomorrow. We will go to railway station and buy your ticket. Daddy you also want to go to St. Thomas. We will book your Air Ticket. Before leaving Ullug, you have to tell Rushdi to pick up my Daddy from Airport. And

Daddy as Akilla has said I and Mom will take care of store while you are away, said Jamshed."

Ullug went to buy ticket along with Jamshed. After getting ticket Ullug called Rushdi! He gave flight details of Ajmal Kureshi and requested him to go to Airport and pick him up. He also gave brief introduction of Ajmal's family and Akilla.

"Ullug! What are you going to do?"

"I will leave this place tomorrow. Good Bye Al Vida."

But Ullug became restless and sad unknowingly.

CHAPTER 17

Zeba During her flight on way back from Turkey was thinking that who can this terrorist be? From photographs he appears to be from a good family. Then can he really spread Virus?. She got tremors and shivers when she got information from people whom she met in Arzuram. To mix Virus in food in such a big function means mass destruction. Those who did not attend the function were saved, but someone or the other from their relations died. Moreover, the way in which children suffered was most inhuman. Due to bloody vomits, bloody stools, heavy fever, cough and cold, children were quite restless and despite the fact that they were laid on an ice slab their fever was not coming down. Due to cough even elderly people suffered and were very uncomfortable. The hospital where they were treated was overcrowded.

Three thousand people died in three days. Such a calamity was never seen before. Initialy it was felt that fever was due to Influenza that has taken place on account of food poisoning, but on chemical investigation it was found that in food, there was Virus-a killing Virus known as "EBOLA". Despite medical treatment, death was a certainty in three days after infection. But how can it be ascertained that same person whose photographs are received did spread Virus?.

And there was a flash in Zeba's mind. Supposing that same terrorist has spread Virus, then the question is why he selected desert area to spread Virus? He must have taken for granted that nobody will come to know about Virus. Then the question is from where he collected Virus? All of a sudden she got a clear picture from the report received by her Director. It was Dr. Wellingdon's report from London. Terrorist must have gone with Russian team to Africa for research. Did someone from that team collected and kept Virus with him? If the photographs are sent to research center in Moscow, can we know about the person?. If the person in photographs is someone from research team, everything will be clear. Further investigations can be done after contacting the Director.

As she was approaching Washington D.C., she was getting more intense to meet Shekhar. How many things were to be discussed with him, and how many of them have already been discussed!. If you cast away the image of Shekhar as a scientist or a scholar or the one doing research, then you will get a picture of a person who is softhearted one having tender feelings. Tired from monotony of his work he used to say to Zeba. "Zeba! You talk about love but the same is a deception in real life. Because of love, eyes of the beloved become tender, wherever you see".

"You will find delicate beauty when you see someone whom you really love. It means in real sense you do not love him/her in totality. Love is an exclusive experience. You can feel it but it is not to be exhibited." I love you!" told once is enough. Repeating the word, I love you is not required. It is just a show. For example from the fragrance, one can know that flower has bloomed. It's fragrance goes with air which does not ask from where fragrance is coming? Why it is coming? It is a matter to be enjoyed. Flower blooms and its fragrance is felt. With fragrance from that flower bees come with a 'Hum' but for that flower does not think anything else, but just enjoy. When you are not there, I become restless and when you are near something or the other is felt. Now you can give any name to my these feelings."

And softly keeping her elbow on table, she used to hear him with sole concentration. She used to enjoy his love and always was keen to see how her love can be expressed in a poem. At that time Zeba used to ask "Shekhar! if someone does not know how to make a poem then.?

"Then there are eyes. In the eyes of the beloved, one can see rising currents of the sea and sail along with them."

"Do you recollect any poem?"

"Yes! I told you that my mother is a poet. My Daddy told me about her in one poem which I will tell you now."

"Does your Daddy also write poems?"

"No! But in love poetry takes shape. Listen what he told to my mother."

"I forget my way and go to your way. Seeing you I become quiet but in your voice there is a sound of cuckoo. I see you and with great delight, I close my eyes and the whole sky of your persona opens up. In that sky, your moon like face brightens up like a lily or lotus. Seeing you I dissolve from myself and I get submerged in you and whole world submerges in it."

She clapped and got delighted at that time. Now while going home, I will ask Shekhar "Do you want to give any name to our relations?" You have to decide and I will surrender my name, my address and myself, all will be submerged in you. I will absolve my eyes in you. I will not have my likes or dislikes for jewelery or lust but I will be all and all in you dissolving my ego".

She got surprised on her poetic thoughts and she realized that with how much intensity she was in love with Shekher. Once her this mission gets over she will say good bye to her present job,she is a woman with desire to have family and children, as she does not want to know classified details so that she would not have to be admitted to that psychic hospital. Showing this photo to Mr. Christie and giving him details, she will tell him about her leaving the job.

An announcement was made that the plane will land soon. Hearing this announcement Zeba was all excited. She went to Shekhar's lab straight from the airport and went to Mr. Christie's office thereafter.

"Come! Come! Totally successful isn't?". Asked Mr. Christie.

"You may take it as a success. It is not a total success but I have a clue."

"Tell me what is it.?"

Zeba took out photo—picture and showed it to Mr. Christie.

Seeing photo Christie asked "Zeba who is he?"

"One new person who reached to the town of Arzuram, but there is no evidence against him."

"This job appears to be difficult. It is sure that deaths occurred by virus as detected. Now it is to be traced that who spread Virus?. It would not have been known it if Dr. Wellingdon's report was not received.

Zeba's eyes brightened.

"Sir! I have one suggestion. Dr. Wellingdon went to Africa for research and found that Chimpanzees died of that Virus only. With Dr. Wellingdon, there were people from other countries too. They must be holding conferences with all of them. If we scan this photo and send the same to him, perhaps he may identify and, if that person was in his research team then he might have spread Virus."

"Very good! I will ring him up and tell him what he has to do. You please scan this photo."

"You ring him up and give full details. I will go to Shekhar's lab and scan this photo and I will come back here. Sir! I want to have some personal matter to be discussed also with you.'

Zeba entered in Shekhar's lab. As usual he was deeply engrossed in his work. He was doing some test. Without disturbing him, she went near his desk and set on a chair. A poem was lying there. She picked it up and started reading.

"The moment I open my eyes, I see your face, I close my eyes and you are in my thoughts. Every drop of my blood repeats your name. In my dreams you wanders. What name should I give to our relations? Just friendship or intense love? My existence depends on you. I want to live for you."

Reading this poem, there was a big flow of love in Zeba. With all the feelings she got up. Slowly she went to Shekhar and embraced him from his back. For a moment Shekhar got a jolt. But seeing Zeba he put down the test and his face brightened up and said "Oh Zeba!, You have come back.?"

"Yes Shekhar! I want to talk to you a lot."

"I also want to talk to you. But did you get any success?"

"Oh Yes! I just forgot, please scan this photo, it is to be sent to Dr. Wellingdon."

Scanning the photo, both of them set on a chair near Shekhar's table.

"Shekhar this is my last mission, once it gets over I am taking retirement."

"Good! Thereafter which new mission you are going to start?" Zeba noticed that seeing her Shekhar was happy.

Getting serious Zeba said "Mission thereafter is to have a family life."

"Did you tell your parents about our relations? What is their response?. Is it good or bad?"

"Wait mianute and so many questions.?"

"Before I tell you, you read this letter."

"Dear Shekhar. We have received your letter. You underestimated both of us. We are educated and we walk with changing times. Who else is in our life except you?. And now in India also Hindu Muslim marriages take place and they are duly accepted. We are not conservative. If both of you are comfortable then what more is needed? Moreover you have all praises for Zeba so much so that we are keen to meet her. You have our blessings, we will come when you say."

Reading that letter, she was quite happy. She got up and embraced Shekhar. She saw that Shekhar was also happy.

"So Shekhar! What do you think now?"

"I have sent them their tickets. Their Visa is quickly arranged by Mr. Christie. My parents have talked to your parents as well. I am waiting for them now."

"I will also talk to Mr. Christie, I will see you later." Saying this Zeba left and she went to Christie's Office. He was seriously thinking something.

"Sir! Are you disturbed?"

"No! I am thinking."

"What did Dr. Wellingdon say?."

"First you take your seat and tell me what you want to say."

"Sir! I want to leave this job after this mission is over." Mr. Christie looked at her for a while and said." Why? After marriage you cannot continue the job.?

"Sir! Do you know?"

"Zeba! You are like my daughter. Shekhar gave me the letter to read, so I have arranged Visas for his parents. I am really happy."

"Sir! I may continue the job after marriage. But in this hectic life how much time can I devote to Shekhar? Now I want to settle down. You are like my friend, so I am telling you that I want to have children." Saying this Zeba blushed.

"Good! We will think about all these things at a later date. First let us talk about our work. Dr. Wellingdon knows this man. He came to Africa in Dr. Khoshev's research team, So there is no doubt about his involvement in this event. But how to nab him without any evidence?. Moreover how to know about his present where about. It will take time but we have to send our agents to inquire".

"Sir! This is my mission. I will carry out investigations but I need your guidance."

"OK!"

The moment Zeba got up there was a telephone ring. Mr. Christie lifted the phone and told to Zeba. "Your Daddy."

"Dear Zeba! When are you coming home? We are waiting for you. Once you come home, we want to give you some news. We have to give it's reply also".

"OK Abbajaan!" Today instead of saying Daddy she called him in a Muslim style and said. "I am coming soon."

While going home she was thinking in her car, what will be the news.? To whom they have to reply? perhaps shekhar'parents?".

CHAPTER 18

Ajmal Kureshi came out of the Airport and saw that Rushdi has come to receive him. Ajmal kept on looking at him. Till now he was thinking that there cannot be a more handsome youth than his son Jamshed. But Rushdi and his childlike innocence drew Ajmal's attention, and he changed his views. Rushdi was having good height, a balanced figure, not very fair and not very dark but he had an attractive face. His eyes were clear without any malice. He was looking quite handsome in Jeans Pant and T-Shirt. He lifted Ajmal's bag with respect and kept it in his car. Ajmal Kureshi asked him about his work. He found Rushdi was having quite a clear thinking. Moreover he got amazed when he saw Rushdi's beautiful residence.

At the entrance of his residence, Fahad Mallick greeted Ajmal Kureshi. "salaam Alekum!" Responding his greetings, Ajmal started enjoying his hospitality. He got amazed seeing the pomp and richness over there. He thought, if Akilla gets married in this family then she will have life long happiness.

All took their seats in living room. Fahad Mallick asked "Ajmal Bhaijaan! What are you doing in Miami'?".

"I have got three convenient stores."

"Do you have to manage everything by yourself?"

"I was doing everything when I was young, but thereafter coming back from the college my son Jamshed used to help me. My wife also was helping me."

"What your son is doing?"

"He is a pilot in Delta Airlines."

"Ajmal Kureshi are you not afraid? At present terrorists are hijacking planes and suicide bombers are traveling with live bombs."

"There is a fear. But nobody ever dreamt that such things will ever happen".

"Ajmal Kureshi you also have a daughter isn't it? What is she doing?"

"She has studied Montessori System of Education in London. We have always liked to see that our children get educated in London. Now she is running a school."

"What are her hobbies?"

"Reading and doing poetry are her other hobbies. She has good control on Urdu language. Her poems are getting published in one monthly magazine published from Hyderabad."

"Are you from Hyderabad?. We are also from that side."

"When did you come over here?"

"After the partition."

"Both your children are born here.?"

"Yes! And they have received education here only, but they care for our cultural values."

"That is our biggest investment."

"This is your—?"

"Yes! He is my only son."

"Rushdi do you know why Ajmal Kureshi has come here?"

"No! Has he come here on a pleasure trip? I will accompany him to show beauty of this place."

There was a smile on Fahad Mallick's face. "Rushdi! He has one daughter."

Rushdie did not understand and looked confused.

"What is your daughter's name?"

"Akilla."

"Good! Rushdi he has brought one proposal for you."

"Abbajaan!" Rushdi got surprized

"Ajmal Kureshi, Fahad Mallick asked. "Have you brought her photograph?"

Taking out her photo from his pocket, Ajmal Kureshi gave it to Fahad Mallick. Seeing the photo he said to his wife. "Mashalla! Begum! it is God's Grace. If in photo she looks so beautiful then how beautiful will she will look when we will see her in person?. Rushdi you please see this photo."

Rushdie took her picture in his hand and stunned by its beauty, kept on looking at it. Her pearly lips were such as if she will speak something right away. Her long cloud like black hair were making her black eyelashes small and pale. A beauty spot on her chin was killing. Rushdi fell in love at the very first sight of Akilla.

"Yes! Rushdi! What do you feel?"

Ajmal Kureshi got surprised when he saw Rushdi getting blushed and he understood that Rushdi has liked Akilla.

"Rushdi there is no hurry for you to reply. Akilla has invited you to Miami. We are not conservative people. You come to Miami, stay with us and meet Akilla. If you feel that both of you can get along well with each other then only we will proceed. Yes! But we do not have mansion like house that you have here." kureshi said

"Ajmal! You have used right word. we need a home and a good heart, not a big mansion. Now we have finished important talks Madam—Begum! what about dinner?." Fahad asked his wife.

"Everything is ready. Please come on the dining table."

While taking dinner, Fahad Mallick asked "When did you meet Ullug?"

"We were together in a flight. He was coming to Miami and I invited him to my place. Do you know? He and his friend Maqsood came to Miami from here only. They came via one cruise ship. Maqsood saved people of the ship from a terrorist. He and Ullug's photos were flashed on T.V."

Hearing Maqsood's name. Fahad Mallick stopped eating. "You said Maqsood? Ullugh and he were together?."

"Yes! Why?"

"You know who is Maqsood? He is a terrorist and right hand of Osama Bin Laden."

Hearing this, food dropped from Ajmal's hands.

"Did Maqsood stay with you?"

"No! He had some other plans."

"But as Ullug was with him and telling him as his friend then perhaps Ullug also . . . . ?"

"No! No! Fahad Mallick he came to purchase diamonds. His parcel came from you only. Taking that parcel he is to go to Washington D.C."

Fahad Mallick was in deep thoughts. Composing himself he said. "Now Rushdi! Tell me when you want to go to Miami and will you get leave from your job?"

"Abbajaan! Ajmal uncle is going to be here for next four to five days and during that time I will arrange for my leave."

As your work is of heavy responsibility if you do not get leave then?

"Abbajaan! Can I make one suggestion?. If I cannot get leave then can we invite Akilla here?"

Fahad Mallick said. "Rushdi do you approve this relationship?".

Rushdi again got blushed. And his face became tender. Ajmal Kureshi saw it and said. "Dear Rushdi I am very fortunate. Now only thing remains to be seen is whether Akilla likes you?. She runs a school, so she cannot close her school and come. But next week, there is a Spring Break so it can be adjusted. After finishing meals I will ring her up."

Dinner got over. Every one came to living room. Ajmal Kureshi called and congratulated his wife Ameena and he also talked to Akilla in detail.

"Abbajaan! From Monday there is a week long Spring Break in my school so if you think fit I can come there."

"Yes dear! You come here and meet every one. We will proceed further only if you say so."

"But Daddy Abbajaan! So long as my Mom has not seen then?"

In the meantime. Jamshed took the phone from Akilla and said. "Daddy! Because of Spring Break, I have also have holidays. I will look after the store. Shall I send Mom with Akilla?"

"Wait a moment", Saying this, Ajmal Kureshi asked Fahad Mallick.

"If you agree can her mother come here along with Akilla?

"Oh! What a great news!. If she comes then the matter can get settled here only. We will announce the engagement and will throw a big party if the boy and the girl agree and if parents concur to it. How do you feel Rushdi?"

Rushdi got lost in dreams to meet Akilla.

"Akilla! Best of luck!" Said Jamshed when he came to airport to see them off. Beautiful face of Akilla got blushed. She was one with very firm determination. She was taking decisions only after deep thinking and planning. She was thinking, if she gets settled in a place nearby then she will not have to go to far off place like Hyderabad in India. What more if she gets a match born and educated in America?. Being of the same community, his parents must have taught him good cultural values.

"Dear Akilla." Hearing her mother calling, she came out of her reverie.

"Yes Mom Ammi!"

"What do you feel from your Abba's talk."

"Mom—Ammi! The boy is well educated and is of friendly nature too. His parents are also well cultured. He is a Research Director in a college lab. So everything appears good to me."

"God may bless Ullug. Though he was not knowing us, he has done a good job."

"Mom! When you are talking about Ullug he appears to be a good man but looks mysterious."

"Why?"

"He was coming to Miami from St. Thomas and that too in a cruise ship then why he sent his parcel in Abba's name?"

"My dear! To keep diamonds with the self is risky isn't it?"

"But Mom! There it is not much checking on cruise ship, even then why he sent the parcel in Abba's name? Can there be something else also in parcel other than diamonds.? I am worried about my Abba. Unnecessarily we will be in trouble. I did not like his his friend also."

"My Dear! Ullug and Rushdi have studied together. They must be knowing each other so you ask Rushdi only about him." And they reached at St. Thomas.

Rushdi, Ajmal Kureshi, Fahad Mallick and his wife all came to receive them. At airport Akilla and her Mom greeted them. Fahad Mallick kept his hand on Akilla's head and blessed her.

Akilla and her Mom liked this gesture. Seeing Rushdi, Akilla was extremely happy, but she continued to hold back her feelings. Fahad Mallick, his wife, Ajmal Kureshi and his wife set in one car and Akilla was asked to accompany Rushdi, so that they can know each other better. While going through the streets of St. Thomas, Rushdi was describing places on the way.

"You are head of one lab over here isn't it?" Akilla asked Rushdi.

"Yes! And you are running a school?"

"Yes!" Said Akilla.

"You are very fond of children isn't it?"

Akilla got startled by such a question from Rushdi.

"I mean in the school there are children only isn't it?".

"Yes! One gets along very well with children."

"Is this your first visit to this place?. Here mountains are worth seeing. This island is small but has many hillocks. Capital city is at the foot of the mountain. So it's mountainous beauty is praised. We will go to that side on our way."

"What are you hobbies.?"

"You might be surprised. I am very much fond of poetry and essays. What about you?"

"I am fond of research work and mountaineering."

"What do you like to read?"

"You might be surprised. My favorite book is" 'The Prophet' of Khalil Gibran. I will like to listen your poem."

Both of them knew each other's choice. In the meantime upward slope came reaching to Rushdi's residence. Akilla saw it with all pleasantness. "Our bungalow is on the hillock" said Rushdi.

Entering in the bunglow, Akilla and her Mom were very impressed. A separate guest room was kept for Akilla. She was happy seeing the furniture and it's arrangement. Ameena went with Ajmal Kureshi to his room. She got pleased seeing sofa, one small T.V. and a fridge in the room. Ajmal Kureshi asked his wife "What do you feel?"

"I am sure you must have liked the bunglow but did you like Rushdi?"

"To be frank, he is quite handsome, well mannered, well educated and easygoing. Where do you get such boys now a days?. I pray to the Allah that Akilla likes him."

"We will talk after dinner."

"After getting fresh, I will go to the kitchen to help Rushdi's mother."

"You also call Akilla for help, so that they can know that Akilla knows cooking."

"OK!" Saying this Ameena went to the kitchen.

Fragrance of Hyderabadi rice was all over in the dinning room.

"Oh! From where the fragrance like this has come after so many years?" asked Fahad.

"I have not prepared, it has been prepared by Akilla" Said Fahad Mallick's wife.

"Oh Dear! I am eating such rice—pillav after many many years" Said Fahad.

"chachajaan! You are praising me to make me feel good, or you are serious." Asked Akilla.

"If you feel so you can ask anyone here, but I am telling you the truth."

Everybody dined happily and went to the living room. Akilla and Rushdi went to portico and set on a swing.

"Did you like my cooking?" Akilla asked Rushdi.

"Excellent! You like our food or something else also."

"As we live in America, dishes like Pizza, Pasta, and Mexican dishes are also liked by me. But I do not like Chinese and Thai food."

"Since I know your taste, now I will keep it in mind."

Fresh breeze was in the air. Akilla's hair lines came down on her forehead. Her hair was also flying gently. In the meantime Rushdi said. "Say one of your poems."

"on what subject?"

"Any subject of your liking?"

"I will say something on atmosphere. Love and beauty have age old liking for each other. It is also life of my life. Today I am experiencing something new. Those who have got satisfaction in this life and do not want anything to be added then they cannot have better life than the life they live. Looking from this angle, I feel that nothing is better than true music. It should come from the sighs of the separation of true lovers."

"This is the poem of Gibran."

Akilla said! "Yes! Since you like Gibran so I said his poem I also like Gibran very much."

Rushdi got overwhelmed looking to Akilla's style of pleasing others. They moved together for quite a some time after that and came closer.

Every one was sitting on the dinning table and both the parents knew from their faces that Rushdi and Akilla have liked each other. So Fahad Mallick asked. "Ajmal Kureshi what do you think now? Shall we confirm relationship?.

"Fahad bhaijaan! my daughter is just like my friend. I will ask her. Come on dear! Do you like Rushdi? Only if you say yes then we will proceed."

Akilla got blushed, keeping her head down and with shyness she said "Yes."

"See! We have got one reply."

"Now you tell Rushdi. Do you like her?"

Rushdi's face got blushed and said "Yes."

"Ajmal! Kureshi you got both the replies." Said Fahad and then he told to Rushdi. "Dear son! Today is Friday. On Sunday Kureshis have to go back to Miami. Tomorrow is Saturday so we will keep function tomorrow. Invite all your friends and relatives and we will make announcement of your engagement with Akilla in the party."

CHAPTER 19

"While going home in her car Zeba waas thinking that the picture given by Mr. Christie, was of a person wearing dress just like Al-Qaeda people. He had beard and mustache. His name was not remembered by Dr. Wellingdon, but he did mention that he was in his research team in Africa. That means virus should have been with him. Where to locate him? What will be his name?.

She reached home in a puzzled mind. Her mother was in kitchen and her father was watching T.V. on Al Zazira channel news about Kuwait. who can forget own motherland! When he saw her, he said "Come in my dearest darling daughter! I want to talk to you quite a few things. He called his wife also. Mr. Khalid was quite elated and was happy. His wife took her seat next to him.

"Dear Zeba! Just think who called?"

"Whose phone came daddy?"

"Your in laws."

"Daddy! I told you I do not want to have any relation with St. Thomas."

"Oh! Since Rushdi is younger to you, I said no to Fahad Mallick. This phone was from your would be in laws."

And Zeba got startled. Little while ago Shekhar also talked about his parents. Reference being made on same topic by her parents, Zeba was happy. At least her parents have accepted her relations with Shekhar.

"Daddy! Please tell me in detail."

"Zeba it seems that you are disturbed. Otherwise I don't think that you cannot understand that I am talking about Shekhar's parents" said Mr.Khalid.

"Now tell me what all was discussed. If they do not agree then why they telephoned?" Though zeba already had read their letter.

"Oh! No! Now it is just the opposite. They were talking about wellbeing of their children. They are coming here this summer. At that time they will meet you and Shekhar."

"Dad!" Zeba being an FBI agent was quite bold and a match for anybody and everybody. But when it came to be a matter of her own engagement and to meet Shekhar's parents as well she was feeling nervous.

"Will they like me? Shall I have to adopt Hindu religion?. Shekhar knows American style of living so I can stay with him. But for his parents shall I have to adopt Hinduism?"

"Dear Zeba! Since childhood I have told you that their God and our God are same. We are praying Him differently and we call Him by different names. If educated class will not understand this, then such mental blocks will never be broken. Basically we are human beings."

"But Dad! Will they understand this?

"Zeba! While talking to them, we felt that they are highly educated. Even not for once they mentioned about religion. They said if both of you are happy then why should there be any objection?." How long we are going to live now?"

Zeba was happy. She already knew their nature and they had accepted her.

"Moreover my dear! We have nothing to say in this matter and you can do whatever you like, but, we will not like you to lose your identity."

"Dad! You are the one with lot of understanding." Saying this Zeba embraced him.

"Zeba! Go to your room, change your agent like dress and come to dining table wearing a woman like dress."

"Mom! Shall I help you?"

"No need! Everything is ready. Come soon."

Seeing Zeba in traditional dress her mother said. "Now you look like a woman."

"Mom! Will they like my wearing such a dress?"

"Zeba! From T.V. channels and T.V. news can you not understand how fast India is progressing.?"

While taking a seat on dining table Zeba said.

"Dad! Mom! How people change with changing times!. Where were we conservative Muslims from kuwait and where are we now staying in this independent life style of America.?"

"Dear! There should not be any objection in adopting good things. So is the country so is the dress. By the way have you met Shekhar?"

"Yes Mom! Yes Dad! I have met him. He is quite happy as his parents are coming here."

"Should be. They are of course his parents. And have you met Mr. Christie.? He was searching something. He had a telephonic conversation with London."

"Yes Dad! It has been traced that people who died in Turkey said to have died due to food poisoning and it was said to be an accident, but truly speaking it was not just a calamity but it was a well planned conspiracy of injecting virus."

"What is the out come?"

"If you have finished your talks shall we sit for dinner?" Asked Zeba's mother.

Zeba further said. "It is pointed to two-three visitors who might have spread virus. One photograph has been received by us and he looks like a terrorist. But what can we do without sufficient evidence?. How to trap him?. His name is also not known. We also do not know where will he be at present? Any news on T.V. Daddy.?"

"Not much. Same news of live bomb explosions, destruction and human loss. I do not know why youngsters get tempted in name of Jehad and get ready to sacrifice their lives." Saying this he pressed remote key of T.V. and opened the channel.

In news they showed photographs taken by media of cruise ship that sailed off from St. Thomas and full report was given of how the ship was saved.

She saw two friends standing near railing of the ship. As the ship reached Miami, media took photos there also. Both friends had very good reception. In zoom camera their faces were clearly seen. Suddenly Zeba pressed 'pause' button.

"Why Zeba? Has the agent within you got something?" Mr. Khalid asked jokingly.

"One minute dad!" She went running to her room and brought the photo given by Mr. Christie and started comparing it with the photo shown in T.V., she said. "Dad please see this photo carefully."

Mr. Khalid attentively looked at the photo but could not find any similarity. Zeba said "Dad! Please keep your palm on his beard and mustache concealing them and see whether both are same or not?"

Mr. Khalid got astonished and said "Oh Zeba! These two faces are quite similar."

"That means the person to whom I and my team are searching is in Miami. Informing Mr. Christie we have to flash this news. Whole exercise will be over once we know his name and his whereabouts in Miami" And she got up.

"Zeba! First you finish your meals and then ring up Mr. Christie" Said Mr. Khalid.

After finishing her meals, Zeba spoke to Mr. Christie giving him full details.

"Zeba you want to complete your mission isn't it?. You take two agents and proceed to Miami, I will inform T.V. to flash that photo in Breaking News slot". Said Mr. Christie.

"Right Sir! But meanwhile i get the flight to go there. In the meantime if he comes to know about this then?"

"You do not lose anything in making efforts."

Zeba turned to Mr. Khalid and said. "Dad! Mom! Mr. Christie is telling me to go to Miami and complete my mission."

"Good! Even otherwise completing this mission you have to pay attention to Shekhar. Get ready for that."

In the meantime phone rang and Mr. Khalid lifted the phone.

"My dear Jamshed" Ajmal Kureshi said in a happy tone. "For our Akilla's engagement, Fahad Mallick has arranged one party and engagement will be announced in that party."

"It means Akilla has agreed."

"My dear son! Rushdi is the one who can be liked by anyone. You will also like him when you will come here and meet him."

"Dad! I will come there by Friday evening flight and return on Sunday. We have to keep our store closed for one day."

"My dear son! It is nothing compared to the happy moments. We all will go back together to Miami on Sunday."

Jamshed came, got settled and soon he met Rushdi. Jamshed was happy of getting a well cultured family of Fahad Mallick for his sister. Seeing the grandeur over there he felt that his sister will be happy. Seeing well lighted bungalow. Jamshed got glimpses of richness of this diamond merchant, but he got clear picture of how influential Mr. Fahad Mallick is during the celebration in which leading people of the community were invited. Invitees got wonder struck seeing well planned dinner and the program thereafter.

"So Akilla! What do you feel? Will you get adjusted here.?"

"My Dear brother! Life definitely gets adjusted when there is mutual understanding."

"Will this philosophy of yours be understood by Rushdi?"

"Dear brother! Please do not take Rushdi as a young man of modern generation. Do you know who is the author of his liking and which book he likes to read?"

"Akilla! You talk about books at this juncture? In this colorful period you should talk about dance and romance."

"Dear Jamshed! You are only two years younger then me. And we are good friends as well. He does not like only books. He knows dancing also quite well. He has learned dancing in London. You will know about him soon."

"That means two of you have made some plans."

"Something like that only. But I will like you to know that author he likes is Khalil Gibran and his book. 'The Prophet' is very much liked by him."

"You have already started taking his side right from now."

"Dear Brother! You will know this only when you will bring someone after you get married."

In the meantime Fahad Mallick got up. He went on the stage where live band was being played. Everyone turned to him. Raising his hands, he started speaking "Ladies and Gentlemen. I welcome you all here, I am sure about one thing that you may be wondering that why all of you are invited here. The reason being today is a very special day for our two families." Saying this he extended his hand to Ajmal Kureshi and invited his family on the stage. Invitees were very happy seeing beautiful Akilla. Fahad Mallick called his wife and Rushdi on the stage. Bringing Akilla and Rushdi in front of the stage he said. "This is Akilla, daughter of Ajmal Kureshi and his wife Ameena from Miami and I announce engagement of my son Rushdi with Akilla."

Living room got resounding noise with claps. Even otherwise the custom is that if you are invited in a function, you cannot go empty handed. So everyone brought something or the other. Everyone came one after another and giving presents, They were blessing the couple. After ceremony got over Fahad Mallick requested all to proceed for dinner.

Dinner had multiple choice. Food was excellent. While taking dinner, people were talking to each other. Rushdi and Akilla were sitting on the dias. Rushdie said "Akilla Madam".

"I will like if you call me Akilla only."

"In that case you have to call me Rushdi."

"OK! But my Mom and Dad will not like that."

"They are not conservative."

"That is true. But that is not our culture. Out of the house we may adopt American style, but within the house we have to honor our culture."

Rushdi felt lucky to get such a wife. As dinner got over, light music started and DJ. announced "Floor is yours."

Rushdi got up and as a host he invited Akilla on the floor. Akilla looked to her parents and other elders. Everyone said 'Yes'. She got up and it was as if bountiful of beauty got up. Rushdi held her hand and both of them went on the floor. Music of waltz started. Both of them were dancing on a low rhythm. Guests were talking that God has created really a nice couple. Other couples started coming on the dancing floor.

Happy and romantic time started up with serene music. Young couples were happily dancing on the floor. Other elders kept on coming to congratulate Ajmal and Fahad.

Suddenly D.J's mobile rang up. He went to the other end of the floor. Suddenly music was stopped D.J. went to Fahad Mallick and said something in his ears. Order was given to switch on T.V. sets kept in the hall. Mr. Christie's face was seen on the T.V. One item in "Breaking the News Slot" was flashed.

"Ladies and Gentlemen Do not get frightened. We want your co-operation. There is going to be terrorist attack on our country. How it will take place is not known. But one terrorist is under screening. He is at present in Miami. His photo will be shown in the T.V. Anyone knowing him should inform us immediately."

Photo was flashed on T.V. Everyone saw it. Slowly party got over. Only Fahad Mallick and Ajmal Kureshi's families were there. They got shivers once they saw the photo, and Fahad looked to Rushdi. He understood.

"Daddy—Abbajaan! It seems there is some misunderstanding."

"Please see with full attention."

Akilla spoke "Daddy" and Ajmal Kureshi got startled.

"Don't you think we know this face?"

"No! Why?"

"Dad—Abbajaan! If he does not have beard and mustache then will his face not look similar to the one shown on T.V."

"Yes my daughter! But how can he be Ullug? Ullug looks like an American."

"Yes! But only if he does not have beard and mustache."

Fahad Mallick immediately said "Look Rushdi this is what I was going to say. Ajmal Kureshi did Ullug come to your place?. Do you know where is he now?"

"Oh Uncle! He must have left for Washington D.C." said Jamshed.

"Why? How?"

"He was to go to Washington D.C. by Sunshine Express train from Miami. To day is Saturday isn't it? He must have left. He was telling he has some important work there on Monday. He has an appointment to go and see White House over there."

Akilla and her mother said "Then we must inform police. If police comes to know later on that he was staying with us we will be in trouble". And they seemed worried.

"Rushdi he was your friend also. You may also get involved. Brother Ajmal we should inform FBI in Home Land Security Dept."

"But Fahad we do not know anybody." Said Ajmal Kureshi.

"You do not worry, I know. Rushdi we have to."

"Yes Abbajaan! But still I am not convinced".

"My dear son! To come out of the clutches of doubts and suspicion there is no alternative but to take such a step."

"OK! Dad—Abbu!"

Fahad Mallick rang up and Mr. Khalid lifted the phone.

Zeba kept on listening her dad talking on the phone.

"Hallo who is there?"

"I am Fahad Mallick from St. Thomas."

"Oh! It's you? "what is the matter?

"Is your daughter Zeba there with you now?"

"We have already talked about her earlier."

"No! No! I do not want to talk in that matter. I have to give you two news. Today we have announced engagement of my son Rushdi with daughter of Ajmal Kureshi of Miami. Other news are about the news flashed on T.V. Please give phone to Zeba I will give her details".

"Hello uncle!" Said Zeba.

"Dear! I want to talk to you in connection with face of a person flashed on T.V. That face is with beard and mustache but by removing the same we fear that one young man with a similar face was our guest at St. Thomas. And from there he went to Miami. You must have heard the news that some one by name Maqsood saved the ship from terrorist. He was an Al-Qaeda man. He killed the terrorist to save his own life. The person whom you want to be traced was with him. We do not know about their relationship".

"He met my son's father in law in the plane and considering him our caste fellow at Miami he invited him to be his guest."

"Then uncle what is his name? Where is he? What are his intentions? Do you know anything about him?"

"His name is Ullug Beg. He is leaving for Washington D.C. today by Sunshine Express train and he will reach Washington D.C. on Monday."

"Uncle how did he meet your relations?"

"Dear! I am giving the phone to him. He will tell you everything. Purpose of ringing you is that he had become guest of our both the families. We do not know anything about his motives."

Fahad gave phone to Ajmal Kureshi. "Hello uncle!. Where did he meet you?".

"Dear he met me while I was returning from Antwerp. He got down at St. Thomas and I went to Miami. From St. Thomas he purchased some diamonds.

He sent that parcel to me at Miami. I got it released from customs."

"But uncle in that parcel there were diamonds only?"

"Dear! I don't know that."

"What luggage he had at the time he left Miami?".

"One suitcase and one back pack. His Washington ticket was also booked by my son."

"Any information about the work he has at Washington?"

"Dear! He was telling that he want to see White House and today he left. We do not know anything about him. Not to have suspicion on us, we rang you up."

"Please don't worry, you have helped me by giving a phone call. Please give the phone to Fahad uncle."

"Uncle congratulations! This information is very important and precious for us."

zeba imediately called Mr.christie, "sir! we are lucky to get all the information about the face on the picture. i knew two Muslim families of St.Thomas and Miami and got all the info. they really helped me. "and she gave all the details.,and said," "sir! he will reach to Washington D.C. on Monday, by train. we would like to intercept him on Potomac river."

"wish you best luck".

when zeba saw back pack in Ullug's hands she visualized those dead people in Turkey. He wanted to kill the president and destroy White house. Before leaving she had informed the details to shekhar and left in a military plane. she had briefed engine driver where to stop the train.

And Ullug got trapped.

CHAPTER 20

"So Ullug! This is your life story; Isn't it? Don't you feel that one incident has misguided you and somebody made you a terrorist?"

"Don't use the word misguided. I have become a terrorist with full awareness. I want to take revenge of Farhana's and caste fellows deaths."

"Just by killing few innocent people?"

"Zeba! Pain that you get by deaths of near and dear ones, these cheaters should also get some idea about that pain."

"Ullug! I have read in Holy Book of Koran that criminals may not be aware of their crimes, so we should forgive them."

"Zeba! I am calling you by your first name because I have sisterly feelings for you. Have you ever fallen in love with anybody?"

Shekhar's affectionate face came before Zeba's eyes. Her face started getting blushed. Ullug got the answer.

"At the time when you lose him or cannot get him, at that time you will understand what is love and pain thereof."

And Zeba started thinking "Will she ever be retiring from this profession and be of Shekhar?" In her mind there was a film that she saw which was about the cobweb of the experience of spying. Will it not dilute her mind? In the meantime Ullug said "OK! Please tell me what will be punishment for my this crime?"

Clearing her thoughts zebe said "If you become our informer then punishment will be less."

"But punishment will be there, Isn't it?"

"Yes! You came to spread terror with an idea to kill the president of America and destroy White House is itself a great crime here but you could not do it. Even then ammunitions of killings have been recovered from you that too the killer ones."

"How do you know that?"

"Ullug! Till now you have not understood how FBI has become number one spying agency in the world?"

"Yes! You came to know from Dr. Wellingdon's report. Isn't it?"

"Moreover from the destruction you did in Turkey."

"How can you say that I have done it?"

"Ullug! You are raw. To start with, you know how corrupt the intelligence department of Russia is? By giving bribe to them you could take out Virus. We also have relations with them. We got detailed report about you. One thing remaining was to trace you. And please do not worry about two Muslim families from St. Thomas and Miami, I know both of them. Come on, think, I will wait for your answer. To enable you to spend your time, I am giving you a book of Al-Mustafa, go through it, I am sure good sense will prevail upon you."

After Zeba left, Ullug got the idea about FBI's net work and he started thinking that by becoming an informer he will get less punishment instead of life imprisonment. By confessing his involvement he will have to spend quite a few years in Jail. How many years? Five, Seven or Ten years or more? What is the use of it? Knowingly or unknowingly I have become a terrorist then is there any purpose in my remaining alive?

One Mr. Maqbool! son of Ullug's distant relative was going to come to meet him. He also believed in Jehad. With great difficulty he requested Maqbool! to bring something for him. How long will it take to get that thing? What should I do?.

His mind was in a whirlpool. He remembered his father and his mind reached to Tashkent. There was a child who was taking his first few steps holding his father's hands. Riding on his father's shoulders he was enjoying horse ride. He could not fulfill his father's ambitions but it was whose fault? Was it not due to fault of Americans? In the meantime Farhana's blushing face came before his eyes as well as her body after the rape. He also remembered his father's death. His face was becoming furious and came in tears. After sometime tears dried up and he took the book in his hand.

Getting composed, he started reading the book.

The best and sweet poetry of love is something like an overflowing peaceful stream of water, sweet, consistent and also witness of endless life. Similarly, the soul also from it's unknown depth making us to listen the love song. But one who takes pleasure from its physical form will get pain and unsatisfied moments he may take as a sublime love. But this approach will kill him. He will never know the freshness of love and without knowing it, his life will come to an end.

"Did he get love from Farhana?"

"Did he submerge her love? Did he fulfill his dad's ambitions?"

His looked at the clock and thought why Maqbool has not yet arrived. Time has ripen to make use of the thing that Maqbool was to bring. Will he be able to cross the security net work? Now there was no escape.

And Maqbool came. While talking, he gave the capsules to Ullug and went away. Again Ullug was in deep thoughts, supposing he may be able to go to his native place after finishing punishment but what next?

But even in prison will Al-Qaeda organization people allow him to live? They don't worry about people like Ullug. For them, he was just a pawn. What difference will it make to them whether I am alive or dead? They will make new terrorists from other young people.

Oh God—Allah! If I would have heard all that was being told by Maulana Khusroo, Fahad uncle, and my daddy, then?

The word "then" made him emotionally upset. Will he be able to live horrible life in jail?. He will be killed if he goes back so shall he stay here only?. In this unknown land?.

"Then? What is the alternative? Suicide?."

taking this decision, he became quiet and serene.

Then he looked at the capsules and said to his life,

"Good Bye!" "Khuda hafeez."

AND Ullug—THE SUN, SET.